"Your brother is a grown man. If he wants to talk to me, I don't see how you can do anything about it."

Taylor's midnight eyes flashed fire. "He's fighting for his life, Wyatt. The last thing he needs is for you to write one of your salacious books about the case and go stirring everybody up all over again. He should be pouring all his energies into his appeal, not wasting his time talking to you."

"I'm sorry you're not happy about it. But as long as he wants to see me, I'll continue going."

"And nothing I can say will change your mind?"

He shook his head. "I'm sorry."

She gazed at him for a long moment, that sweetly curved mouth tight and angry; then she turned and stalked away, leaving him with his head pounding and unwilling guilt gnawing at his insides.

Dear Reader,

We keep raising the bar here at Silhouette Intimate Moments, and our authors keep responding by writing books that excite, amaze and compel. If you don't believe me, just take a look RaeAnne Thayne's *Nothing To Lose,* the second of THE SEARCHERS, her ongoing miniseries about looking for family—and finding love.

Valerie Parv forces a new set of characters to live up to the CODE OF THE OUTBACK in her latest, which matches a sexy crocodile hunter with a journalist in danger and hopes they'll *Live To Tell.* Kylie Brant's contribution to FAMILY SECRETS: THE NEXT GENERATION puts her couple *In Sight of the Enemy,* a position that's made even scarier because her heroine is pregnant—with the hero's child! Suzanne McMinn's amnesiac hero had *Her Man To Remember,* and boy, does *he* remember *her*—because she's the wife he'd thought was dead! Lori Wilde's heroine is *Racing Against the Clock* when she shows up in Dr. Tyler Fresno's E.R., and now his heart is racing, too. Finally, cross your fingers that there will be a *Safe Passage* for the hero and heroine of Loreth Anne White's latest, in which an agent's "baby-sitting" assignment turns out to be unexpectedly dangerous—and passionate.

Enjoy them all, then come back next month for more of the most excitingly romantic reading around—only in Silhouette Intimate Moments.

Yours,

Leslie J. Wainger
Executive Editor

Please address questions and book requests to:
Silhouette Reader Service
U.S.: 3010 Walden Ave., P.O. Box 1325, Buffalo, NY 14269
Canadian: P.O. Box 609, Fort Erie, Ont. L2A 5X3

Nothing To Lose

RAEANNE THAYNE

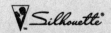

INTIMATE MOMENTS™

Published by Silhouette Books

America's Publisher of Contemporary Romance

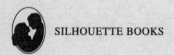 **SILHOUETTE BOOKS**

ISBN 0-373-27391-6

NOTHING TO LOSE

RAEANNE THAYNE

lives in a graceful old Victorian nestled in the rugged mountains of northern Utah, along with her husband and two young children. Her books have won numerous honors, including several readers' choice awards and a RITA® Award nomination by the Romance Writers of America. RaeAnne loves to hear from readers. She can be reached through her Web site at www.raeannethayne.com or at P.O. Box 6682, North Logan, UT 84341.

Chapter 1

"*A family shattered, innocence destroyed. The tragic death of Cassie Nyland reminds us once more that the monsters we should fear most are those that lurk inside ourselves.*"

Enthusiastic applause burst through the bookstore just off the University of Utah campus when Wyatt McKinnon closed the pages of his latest book. He offered the audience the smile the writer for *Vanity Fair* had called "dangerously enigmatic" at the same time he fought the urge to rub at the familiar tension headache pounding holes in his temples and his concentration.

He hated speaking in public. After ten book tours, he probably should be used to it. But no matter how many readings he gave like this one—how many speeches, how many television interviews—he couldn't shake the feeling that it was all a mistake, that eventually everyone would figure out he was just a hick cowboy from Utah who didn't deserve any of the wide acclaim that had found him after the publication of his first book, *Shadow of Fear.*

Only neurotic-writer blues, he told himself again and straightened his spine to face the crowd of university students suddenly clustering around him. They all looked so young, pathetically eager, and he had the lowering thought that they were all barely in elementary school when he finished college himself a decade earlier.

"That was *so* wonderful, Mr. McKinnon." A perky brunette with a tight gymnast's body and a brilliant smile that must have set her parents back a small fortune in orthodonture was the first in line. "Your books are all *so* scary. I can't pick one up unless my roommate is home. They're scary but *so* gripping, you know?"

"I'm pleased you think so," he responded automatically.

"Oh, I do. Will you sign *Blood Feud* for me?" She thrust a copy of a book he was currently promoting. "To Brittanee, with two E's."

With a dutiful smile, he signed the book, then spent the next hour doing his best to keep that smile firmly in place while his headache cranked up a couple of dozen notches and the muscles in his hand cramped from all the books he signed.

Finally the crowd dispersed, until only a few people remained. One was Paul Cambridge, an old college friend whose family owned the bookstore. He was talking to one of the salesclerks and held up a finger to let Wyatt know he was almost ready to take him out for the seafood enchiladas at Cafe Pierpont as he had promised.

Wyatt nodded and rose to stretch, then caught sight of a woman he had noticed briefly earlier. She hadn't moved from the back row of chairs. Now that he had a moment to focus on her more closely, he thought she looked vaguely familiar.

He narrowed his gaze. It wasn't until she rose and approached him that all the pieces clicked together.

"Taylor Bradshaw, right?" he said quickly as she came to stand before him.

A flare of some unreadable emotion registered briefly in eyes a deep and lovely blue, but she quickly veiled it. "Yes."

The last time he had seen her was during the sentencing phase of her brother's murder trial eighteen months earlier. When Hunter Bradshaw had been sentenced to death by lethal injection for the murder of his girlfriend, her mother and her unborn fetus, the former Salt Lake City police detective hadn't so much as blinked in reaction.

Bradshaw's sister had been a different story. When Judge Leonis had pronounced the grim sentence, every trace of color had leached from the elegant, fragile features of Taylor Bradshaw and she had collapsed to the floor of the courtroom.

That small scene had been just one more in a string of dramatic developments in the case that had captivated the public's interest. Successful, popular television personality murdered by the father of her unborn baby. It was a fascinating case and Wyatt couldn't wait to finish his research and start writing about it.

He didn't wonder that he hadn't immediately recognized Taylor Bradshaw. Except for some shadows lingering in those huge blue eyes, the woman standing in front of him barely resembled the pale, distressed young woman who had haunted the courtroom every day.

She also didn't look much like the other college students who had attending his reading, in their jeans and T-shirts and slouchy backpacks. Taylor Bradshaw wore tailored slacks and a russet blazer over a crisp white shirt. She carried a leather briefcase and exuded an air of professional competence. Her auburn hair was cut shorter than he remembered it and her face was harder, somehow. Determined.

She looked…driven. He couldn't come up with another word to describe her. He knew she had been in her last year of medical school during the trial and he wondered now if she had returned to finish up. He sincerely hoped for her sake that she had. Just because her brother was living on borrowed time didn't mean she had to shove her own life into the deep freeze.

"I'm surprised to see you here," he admitted.

Her gaze was as cool as the October night outside the bookstore. "I'm sure you are."

Though both of them had attended the monthlong trial every day, they had spoken only once. It hadn't been a friendly conversation, Wyatt remembered with an internal grimace. During a recess in the trial, he had slipped to the coffee shop across the street from the courthouse and discovered Taylor sitting alone in a quiet corner booth.

He remembered she had some kind of thick medical textbook propped up in front of her, but over the top of it he had just been able to see her eyes. The utter lack of hope in them still haunted him.

That despair had changed to bitter anger when he approached her booth, driven by some insane desire to try to comfort her.

"Looking for a scoop, Mr. McKinnon?" she had asked, her tone biting.

"No. Just a lunch companion. I hate eating alone." But even his friendliest smile didn't thaw the chill in her eyes by a single degree.

She snapped shut her textbook and slid out of the booth. "Too bad. I'm done here."

The full plate of food in front of her gave the lie to her

words and made him annoyed at his own foolishness. She didn't want his comfort. What had he expected, that she would be thrilled to have his company?

"Come on, don't run away. You have to eat. I won't bother you, I promise."

"I've suddenly lost my appetite. Something about yellow journalism does that to me."

The denunciation had stung, he had to admit. He took pride in his work, in presenting the blunt truth, no matter how unpalatable it might be. Through his career he had received thanks not only from the families of the victims he wrote about but also the families of their killers for helping them understand what had gone so horribly wrong.

Before he could respond to Taylor Bradshaw's derisive comments, she had stalked out of the diner, and she had studiously avoided him for the remaining days of the trial.

Apparently the intervening eighteen months hadn't softened her attitude toward him at all. She still looked at him like she thought he was approximately as appealing as a cow with the slobbers.

"Hunter told me you've been going to the Point of the Mountain to see him."

"A few times, yes."

"He told me he's cooperating with you from prison on the book you're writing about his case."

"We've had a few conversations, mostly about his relationship with Dru Ferrin. How they met, how long they dated, that sort of thing."

"I don't want you going out there again."

Wyatt studied the muscle flexing along her jawline and the hot color climbing her cheekbones. He wasn't the kind of man to go looking for fights but he wouldn't back down when one found him, either. "Your brother is a grown man, Ms. Bradshaw," he murmured. "If he wants to talk to me, I don't see how you can do anything about it."

Anger snapped to life in her eyes. "I can ask you to have a little human decency, if you even know what that is. My brother is living in hell. The last thing he needs is for you to write one of your salacious books about the case and go stirring everybody up all over again."

In the court of public opinion, Hunter Bradshaw had been guilty of the Ferrin murders before he ever walked into that courtroom. In conservative Utah, where Dru Ferrin had been a pretty, popular television personality, and with the case involving the violent deaths of pregnant women or their terminally ill mothers, the man hadn't stood a chance of being acquitted.

"I'm not trying to stir everybody up again," he said, deciding to ignore that whole "salacious" bit. "All I want to do is explore a little more deeply why it happened."

"To know why Dru and her mother were killed, don't you think you have to know who really did it first? It certainly wasn't my brother."

"A jury of his peers said he did."

"That jury was wrong! And if you write a book saying he killed anyone, all you will be doing is furthering their injustice."

"Your faith in your brother is admirable, Ms. Bradshaw."

"Admirable but misplaced. That's what you're thinking, isn't it?"

That was exactly what he'd been thinking but he didn't have the heart to voice his opinion. "He *was* convicted," Wyatt pointed out gently. "Hunter is on death row. In the eyes of the courts and the world, he's guilty of killing both women and Dru's unborn child."

"I don't care what the world says. I know he didn't do it! My brother is facing *death* for something he didn't do. What could be worse?"

Despite his own knowledge of the case and the overwhelming avalanche of evidence against Bradshaw, Wyatt couldn't help being stirred by the force of her convictions.

Taylor went on. "You've met him. Can you honestly tell me you think he's capable of this crime?"

That was one of the things that bothered him most about this case, Wyatt had to admit. Bradshaw was a tough man to peg. He had a reputation for being a smart, dedicated cop. Stubborn enough to earn his share of enemies on the force, but passionate about the job and not at all the sort who would fly into a rage and kill two women.

During their three prison interviews, he had seen none of that passion the prosecution had alleged. Bradshaw had been courteous but cool, showing no emotion whatsoever.

Wyatt wasn't being arrogant to acknowledge that one of the reasons his books had been so well-received was his ability to climb inside the minds of the killers he wrote about. As uncomfortable as he found such places, the perspective always gave a rich depth to his writing, a gritty verity he worked hard to attain. But Hunter Bradshaw wasn't letting him anywhere near his mind. The man he met was as remote and cool as the Yukon.

"Who knows what any of us is capable of with the right provocation?" he responded.

Taylor Bradshaw's midnight-blue eyes flashed fire. "I don't know you. I don't know what you're capable of. But I do know my brother and I know he would never lift a finger to hurt any woman, especially not the woman he thought was carrying his child."

Wyatt thought again of Dru Ferrin, the girl he'd known in

grade school, pretty and sassy and smart-mouthed. He'd been lost and terribly lonely when he returned to Utah with his mother after the divorce. Missing his dad and Gage like crazy, mourning Charlotte, traumatized by the purgatory they had all been through.

The other children hadn't known how to talk to him— what did a nine-year-old say to a kid who was the only witness to his little sister's kidnapping?—but Dru had always been kind to him.

For that alone, he wanted to write her story, so he could remember that girl willing to sit by him on the school bus when everybody else treated him like he had head lice.

"Leave Hunter alone." A pleading note crept into Taylor's voice and her hand tightened on her attaché. "He's fighting for his life. He should be pouring all his energies into his appeal, not wasting his time talking to you."

"I'm sorry you're not happy about it. But your brother seems to want to tell his side of the story. As long as he wants to talk to me, I'll continue going down to the Point of the Mountain."

"And nothing I say will change your mind?"

He shook his head. "I'm sorry," he said again.

She gazed at him for a long moment, that sweetly curved mouth tight and angry, then she turned and stalked away, leaving him with his head pounding and unwilling guilt gnawing at his insides.

Taylor was greeted by two things a half hour later when she let herself into her little house in the Avenues—the rich smell of something Italian and spicy wafting from the kitchen, and a huge furry shape that rushed her the moment she walked inside.

Belle's eager welcome went a long way to helping Taylor shake the anger and frustration that lingered from her encounter with Wyatt McKinnon.

She dropped her case and gave the dog the obligatory attention, ignoring the hair Belle eagerly deposited. "Yeah, I'm happy to see you too, you crazy dog, even if my jacket will never be the same. How was your day, sweetheart? Anything exciting happen?"

"Not much. I worked a double shift at the hospital, then got hit on by the kid who bagged my groceries."

Taylor turned her attention from the Irish setter she had inherited from Hunter after his arrest to her roommate and best friend standing in the doorway. "Big surprise." She grinned. "You get hit on by everyone."

"Not true. Only sixteen-year-old bag boys and sixty-year-old anatomy professors. Nobody date-able." Kate's rueful grimace did nothing to hide her model-beautiful features.

At the wry reference, Taylor had to laugh as she remembered Andrew McLean, the anatomy professor in question who had been notorious for propositioning all of his female medical students. Even Taylor had been on the receiving end of one of Randy Andy's absymal pickup lines.

It seemed like another lifetime ago when she met Kate Spencer on the first day of McLean's anatomy class, when they'd been paired up as lab partners. Both of them had been first-year medical students, overwhelmed and a little lost by the new world they'd been thrust into.

Recognizing kindred spirits, they had become immediate friends and study partners. Both of them had the same fierce dedication toward medical school, with little interest in anything but succeeding and becoming physicians.

During their second year of med school, Taylor's father

died of a massive heart attack after walking out of the courtroom where he presided with the same iron fist and cold re-
solve he had shown to his children.

After his death, she purchased this house near the university with part of her inheritance. Though she could have gotten by financially without a roommate, she discovered after
a few months that she didn't like living alone. Kate had been
the logical choice.

They had shared so much together, Taylor thought now as
she studied her roommate. Hopes and dreams and late-night
cram sessions and a memorable cross-country trip one spring
break to visit Kate's foster parents in Florida.

They would have graduated together the previous year if
Hunter's arrest hadn't plowed like a freight train through Taylor's educational plans. While Kate had finished up and was
now a second-year resident at University Hospital, Taylor's
life had taken a drastic turn.

She had withdrawn from her last semester of classes to attend the trial. After Hunter's conviction, she had dropped out
of medical school altogether. Now, instead of anatomy and
physiology, she was immersed in torts and civil procedure.

She shook off the depression that suddenly settled on her
shoulders like a weighted cloak at the reminder of the mounds
of homework awaiting her before she could sleep.

"So how was the lecture?" Kate asked. "Did you get a
chance to talk to the evil Wyatt McKinnon?"

"I spoke with him," she said grimly.

"And?"

"He's not budging."

"Did you really expect him to drop the whole project just because you asked him to? He was there every day of the trial too."

She sighed, slipping off her shoes and hanging her blazer

in the closet off the entry. "Not really. Still, it was worth a shot. I guess I just wanted to make sure he knows how strongly I object to the idea of him making money off the hell Hunter is going through."

"I'm not sure the money is all that important to him. He's had ten books at the top of the bestseller lists. I think if Wyatt McKinnon never wrote another word, he would still be worth millions."

Rich and successful and gorgeous. The man had everything. Her mouth tightened again. Why did he affect her so strongly? She should despise him for what he was doing to Hunter. She *did,* she assured herself.

So why had she sat through his reading as captivated by his words as every other brainless coed in that bookstore? Something about Wyatt McKinnon's lean, rangy build and his tanned features and the intensity in his sage-green eyes seemed to reach right inside her and tug out feelings she had never imagined lurked inside her.

She could never tell Kate that. If her roommate ever figured out she was attracted to the blasted man, Taylor would never hear the end of it.

By unspoken agreement, the two women headed for the kitchen, Belle padding along behind them. Kate returned to the stove and stirred a tomato sauce bubbling there while Taylor set out plates and silverware.

"I read that article about him in *Vanity Fair* a few months ago," Kate went on. "It might have been hype, but I got the impression he's not in it for the money."

"I'm sure he doesn't turn it away when his publisher sends him all those big fat royalty checks."

"Maybe not, but I think there's more to it than that. Hang on a minute."

Kate set the spoon down with a clatter and suddenly dashed out of the kitchen toward her bedroom, Belle following on her heels. A moment later she rushed back and thrust a magazine at Taylor.

Gazing back at her out of those vivid green eyes that gleamed behind wire-rimmed glasses was none other than Wyatt McKinnon, wearing cowboy boots and a denim jacket and looking as if he had just climbed off the back of a horse.

"I thought I still had this—"

Though Taylor wasn't sure how Kate could look at anything but that compelling picture, her roommate scanned the article.

"Here is that quote I was looking for, about why he writes what he does."

She pulled the magazine away from Taylor and read out loud. "'I write for the victims and the victims' loved ones. When a family loses someone through a violent crime or an unsolved disappearance, their lives are changed forever. The world is never again as shiny and bright with possibilities. Though it doesn't take away any of their pain, victims' families deserve to know the truth about what happened and, more importantly, to know their lives won't be forgotten.'"

"He sounds as if he *knows*. I wonder if he's lost someone." Taylor studied the picture, looking for shadows behind that enigmatic smile. She couldn't tell anything from the glossy photograph.

"The article doesn't say anything like that about him, but it's possible." Kate returned to the stove to drain the pasta. For a few moments the kitchen was silent except for Belle's snuffly breathing and the sauce burbling on the stove.

"You know," Kate said suddenly, "maybe you've been going about this the wrong way with McKinnon."

"How?"

"You want to keep him from interviewing Hunter. But maybe you should be thanking your lucky stars he's interested in the case."

Taylor stared at her. "You're crazy. Hunter doesn't need more negative publicity. He's had enough to last a lifetime."

"What if it's not negative? McKinnon's books are extensively researched. He has a reputation for writing genuine, accurate stories, even in cases where the cops messed up. If you show him the evidence you've gathered since Hunter's conviction, he can't help but see that your brother is innocent."

"You're the one who read that quote. He writes for the victims and their families. Not for the accused killers."

"We both know Hunter is no killer. You just have to convince Wyatt McKinnon. Imagine what it would do for Hunter's appeal if McKinnon wrote a book questioning whether an innocent man is on death row!"

"He sat through the trial and heard the state's case. As far as he's concerned, Hunter killed Dru and her mother and her unborn baby. Just like the rest of the world, I'm sure he thinks Hunter deserves what's coming to him."

"You just have to prove that he and the rest of the world are wrong."

Taylor gave a short laugh. "Sure. And while I'm at it, I'll solve world hunger and in my spare time maybe I'll find a cure for cancer."

"Who else will speak up for Hunter? You and I are just about the only people on the planet who believe he's innocent. But imagine if he had someone as influential and well-known as Wyatt McKinnon in his corner. He would be bound to win an appeal."

Kate was right. If she could somehow convince Wyatt to

help her prove her brother didn't murder anyone, it would undoubtedly help Hunter's appeal. But how could she face him
again? Just the idea of another encounter made her stomach
hurt worse than the first time she had to answer a question
aloud in her miserable contracts-law class.

She could do it, though. She *would*. Hunter's life de-
pended on it.

Chapter 2

Taylor dreaded Tuesday afternoons like she used to hate the dance lessons her father insisted on during her pre-adolescence.

Monday evening at around nine o'clock her stomach would start to ache like a rotten tooth and her shoulders would stiffen with tension. She could pretend everything was fine, could just go on as normal and try her best to concentrate through her Tuesday morning torts class. But by the time she set off on the thirty-minute drive from the University of Utah campus to the Point of the Mountain state prison, at the south end of the vast Salt Lake Valley, she was usually a mass of tangled nerves.

Hunter really didn't want her there. Each visit he told her not to come again, to contact him by phone if she needed to talk to him. But each Monday evening she girded herself for the ordeal of another visit.

She hated it, but she would keep coming every Tuesday until hell froze over, or until Hunter was free.

As horrible as it was to see her brother under the harsh, de-humanizing conditions at the prison—to watch him harden a little more each week—she knew she would continue to make this trip across the valley, past housing developments and shopping malls and warehouses.

If nothing else, each visit to her brother's hell renewed her determination to see him out of there.

She drew in a deep breath and fought the urge to press a hand to her knotted stomach as she watched the mile markers slip past.

When she was younger, her father had taken her and Hunter this way a few times on business trips out of the valley to southern Utah or Las Vegas. She had never given it much thought, other than to wonder at this scary huddle of buildings that seemed out in the middle of nowhere.

She found it disconcerting to realize how in eighteen months the Point of the Mountain complex had become so much a part of her life.

The valley's population had grown dramatically in the past decade and houses had sprung up within a stone's throw of the prison complex. Draper and Bluffdale were two of the fastest-growing communities in the state. How odd, she thought, that South Mountain, to the east of the prison across the freeway, was actually one of the more desirable slices of real estate in the valley, with sprawling, million-dollar homes and groomed golf courses.

She wondered if Hunter could look across the interstate at all those bright, shiny houses—if the contrast between the world of those who lived in them and his own life seemed as stark and depressing to him as it always did to her.

She took the prison exit and a few moments later passed the first of many security checkpoints. The guard recognized her but checked her driver's license against his visitor list anyway, before allowing her to enter. Cars weren't searched entering the prison—only on the way out.

In the visitor parking lot, she sat for a moment behind the wheel, trying to dig deep inside herself for at least the semblance of a positive attitude. For Hunter's sake, she tried hard to hide how much she hated coming here, how each visit seemed to bleed away more of her hope that her brother would walk free.

Just for practice, she forced a smile for the rearview mirror. Okay, it wasn't exactly perky but it was better than nothing.

With her non-perky smile firmly in place, she locked her car, pocketed her keys—since purses weren't allowed inside—and headed into the Uinta maximum security prison for the next round of checkpoints.

The guard waiting inside was the first bright spot in what had been a grim day. He offered her a wide, sunny smile. "Doc Bradshaw. This is a pleasure."

Her smile felt almost genuine as she greeted Richard Gonzolez. She didn't bother to correct him that she was several credits shy of ever being a doctor. He had called her Doc Bradshaw as long as she had been coming to see her brother.

Richard was one of her favorite guards in the unit—some of the corrections officers made her feel even more like a piece of meat than did the leering inmates, but Officer Gonzolez always treated her with courtesy and respect and even kindness.

"Great to see you again!" she said. "I've missed you these last few months. I thought Tuesdays were your day off."

"I'm back on for a while. I needed to change my shift so I could have Fridays off instead."

"How's Trina?" Taylor asked about his wife.

His ready smile looked a little strained around the edges.

"Could be worse, I guess. She was tired of her hair falling out in clumps so she shaved it all last week. I told her it looks sexy—told her I was gonna get her a belly ring and a tattoo and take her down to the Harley-Davidson shop for some leathers so she'd look like a biker chick."

"I guess she didn't go for that."

"Not my Trina." He met her gaze and the worry in his brown eyes made her heart ache. "She tries to stay upbeat for me and the kids but it's been tough on her. That's why the shift change. She's onto her second round of chemo and they changed the day to Fridays. I didn't want her to do that on her own."

A dozen questions crowded through her mind—Trina's white blood cell counts, her med regimen, how she was doing emotionally after her radical mastectomy—but she managed to clamp down on them. Despite Richard's affectionate nickname for her, she wasn't a doctor. An almost-doctor, maybe, but she hadn't been part of that world for a long time.

"Trina is in good hands with Dr. Kim. He's the best around."

"That's one of the things that keeps her going. We both know we never would have gotten in to see him if it hadn't been for you."

Taylor just shook her head. "I didn't do anything, only pulled a few strings."

"Well, we sure appreciate it."

Under other circumstances, she would have given his hand a reassuring squeeze, but she knew this wasn't the time or place. "Please let me know how things are going."

"I sure will," he said, with a smile that filled her with shame at her own self-pity.

This kind man's wife was waging a fierce, losing battle against breast cancer and he could still manage to smile. All she had to do was spend an hour in a place she loathed. Surely she could be at least as cheerful as Richard Gonzolez.

"Sorry to tell you this," the guard said, "but you'll have to wait a few minutes. Your brother already has a visitor in the last group. Time's almost up, though."

That was odd. Hunter rarely had visitors besides her. They had no other family and her brother had never been much of a pack animal. Most of his so-called friends had abandoned him after his arrest. She wondered who it might be.

"I don't mind waiting," she assured the guard, then took her seat with the other visitors waiting their turn.

She had never been very good at coping with unexpected blocks of free time. Usually she tried to carry around at least one law book at all times so she could use her time constructively and keep up with her reading lists—probably a holdover from the judge's frequent edicts against wasting time.

In this case, she had no choice, as she'd left all her books in her car. She picked up a news magazine and tried to leaf through it but found little of interest.

She was trying a woman's magazine—with much the same malaise—when the volume in the room increased as the previous group of visitors was led out.

She recognized a few familiar faces and was once more struck by how insular this prison community could be. She had watched people make friendships, business connections, even romances while they waited to visit someone on the inside.

A few minutes later, she had risen to wait her turn to go into the visiting area when a familiar face appeared in the crowd—this one unexpected.

Wyatt McKinnon walked out, looking tall and lanky and gorgeous.

The same reaction she'd had to him the other times they'd

met started stirring around inside her. The same butterflies in her stomach, the same silly breathlessness, the same surge of awareness.

What was the *matter* with her? This wasn't at all like her. She just wasn't the kind of woman to lose brain cells over a man. Especially not *this* man—and especially not in these circumstances.

She drew in a deep, steadying breath. He hadn't seen her yet, she realized as she watched him stop to exchange words with one of the guards—not Richard but another she had met only a few times.

Wyatt greeted the man with a ready smile, though from here it looked as if it dimmed a little when the corrections officer produced a book from beneath the desk. From here she could see it was Wyatt's latest bestseller. The guard wanted it signed, she realized, just like all those silly little coeds who had flocked to the lecture the other night.

She couldn't be too derisive of them, she thought with brutal self-honesty. Not with her pulse skipping and this weak trembling in her stomach.

Wyatt signed the book with a flourish, handed it back to the guard with a polite smile, then turned to leave.

She knew exactly the moment he noticed her. Surprise flickered in those grey-green eyes and he froze for an instant, then walked toward her.

"Taylor. Ms. Bradshaw. I didn't realize your brother had another visitor waiting. I'm sorry—I'm afraid I went a little long. I hope I didn't take all your time."

A few days earlier she might have given him some sharp reply about how her time was just as valuable as his, but she decided that wouldn't be diplomatic, not if she still wanted his help.

In theory, Kate's idea had seemed a good one. Wyatt McKinnon could be a powerful ally. His words had influence, and she had just seen more evidence that he had readers everywhere. If she wanted his help, she knew she would have to ask for it. But being confronted by the man made her tongue feel as slippery as a hooked trout.

"He's still allowed another half hour of visitation." She sucked in a breath for courage. "Listen, I..."

Richard cut her off. "Doc Bradshaw, you're up. You ready to go back?"

She rose, aware as always of the time and how limited it was.

She had learned since Hunter's arrest that life behind bars was ruled by the clock. Inmates talked of marking time, doing time, hard time. Their world revolved around the tick of each passing second.

"Look, I've got to go or I'll miss my chance. Would you mind...that is, um—" she faltered. Oh, this was hard! She would rather be foxtrotting with the sweaty-palmed Troy Oppenheimer who had been the bane of her dance-class days than be forced to grovel to Wyatt McKinnon.

But she had no choice.

"Would you mind waiting for me?" she asked in a rush. "I...I need to talk to you."

His eyebrows rose in surprise but he nodded. "Of course. I'll be here when you come out."

The guard led her to one of the visitor chambers. In the maximum security unit, visits were always non-contact and were carried out in individual rooms separated by a Plexiglas divider.

Hunter was already on the other side of the glass, dressed in the obligatory orange jumpsuit. His dark, wavy hair could use a trim and he had a bruise along his jawline that hadn't been there the week before.

He looked big and mean and dangerous, and she grieved all over again for the dedicated, passionate cop he had been.

He didn't smile when he saw her, but she thought perhaps his eyes softened a little. She wanted to believe they did, anyway, though she thought that was probably just more self-delusion.

Every time she visited him, Hunter seemed a little colder, a little more remote. Hard and brittle, like a clay sculpture left to dry too long in the broiling sun.

She was so afraid that one Tuesday she would discover nothing left of him but a crumbled pile of dust.

"What happened to your jaw?" she asked after she sat down and picked up the phone.

That jaw tightened. "Nothing. I slipped in the yard while I was shooting hoops one day."

He was lying. She had grown up with him, had seen him butting heads with the judge during his rebellious years often enough to recognize the signs. But she also knew he would choke on his own tongue rather than tell her what really happened.

Former cops—especially homicide detectives—didn't exactly make the most popular prison inmates. She knew there were plenty of other inmates he had helped put behind bars who probably weren't too thrilled to have Hunter Bradshaw join them in the pen. And though he would never say anything about it, she also knew most of the guards treated him with a contempt and derision reserved for one of their rank who had gone bad.

Oh, how she hated this. She hid her sisterly concern and brought out that smile she had practiced in her car earlier, though it felt cheesier than usual.

"I ran into Wyatt McKinnon out in the visitor waiting room. How often is he coming to talk with you?"

His sigh came over the phone loud and clear. "Don't start in on this again, Tay."

"What? I didn't say anything."

"No, but you have that *what the hell are you thinking?* look on your face."

"You're imagining things. Must be the lighting in here."

"Lighting my ass. I know what you think about McKinnon."

Don't be so sure, she wanted to say but held her tongue.

Hunter went on. "He told me you went to see him last week. He said you asked him not to write the story."

Okay, it had been a lousy idea. She had known it even before she went to the bookstore, but she had never been very good at inaction. When something was wrong in her world, she tried to take steps to fix it.

"It didn't do much good, did it? He's still here today."

"You think I'm crazy to talk to him, don't you."

She thought of all her many objections to Wyatt writing a book about the case. Her biggest fear was that it would make life even harder for Hunter here behind bars.

"I don't think you're crazy," she answered. "I just hope you know what you're doing."

"Somebody's going to write the story. We both know it's only a matter of time. I'm surprised nobody has done it yet. If not McKinnon, it will be someone else, and frankly, I prefer him to some of the bottom-feeders who've tried to get interviews with me. McKinnon talked to me a few times about other cases when I was on the job and actually quoted me correctly. From what I've seen of his work, I figure he'll at least try to be fair. He cared enough to attend the trial, not just rely on court transcripts."

"That's true. He was there every day. I wonder why he's just now writing the story."

"A few reasons, I suppose. I only decided to talk to him a few months ago and I do know he had to finish another project before he could write this one." He paused. "Today he told me he would like to talk to you. I'm sure he wants to know what it was like growing up with a vicious killer."

"I wouldn't know," she shot back quickly.

Hunter's short laugh echoed in the phone. That was why she continued these torturous visits. If she could make him laugh even once, everything was worth it.

"Will you talk to him?"

She sighed. "I already planned to. He's waiting for me to finish up my visit."

"Really?"

"Kate seems to think convincing Wyatt McKinnon you're innocent might help your appeal. I would like to show him all the evidence that was thrown out at trial that proves you could never have killed anyone."

He shook his head in resignation, but there was a warmth in his eyes that she hadn't seen in a long while.

"You never did know when to give up the fight, did you. Remember when you brought home that stray mutt and the Judge said under no conditions would that mangy thing ever be allowed in our house? You hid him at Suzie Walker's house down the street and spent weeks wearing the Judge down."

She smiled at the memory. "I think what finally did the trick was the ten-page research paper I did—complete with footnotes and annotations—outlining how child development experts believe pets can be beneficial to young minds."

"That's funny. I thought it was the amateur ad campaign you shot of you taking care of Rascal down at Suzy Walker's—feeding him, walking him, teaching him tricks."

"I miss that dog. You know, he would have died before admitting it but I think the Judge warmed up to Rascal eventually. After you moved out, I even caught him petting him a few times."

Hunter unbent enough to smile—or as close as he came to a smile these days anyway. Too quickly, though, he sobered. "You're not going to win this one, Tay. You need to face facts here. God knows, I have. Life is a hell of a lot easier to deal with after you stop holding on to foolish hope."

"Without hope, what else do you have?"

He didn't answer, but she saw the truth in the bleakness of his eyes. Nothing. He had nothing. She wouldn't have thought it possible but her heart cracked apart a little more.

Before she could respond, the guard walked up behind Hunter. "Time's up," he said, his features stony.

Oh, she hated time, especially each reminder that it was quickly running out.

"I haven't given up hope," she said urgently into the phone, wishing more than anything that she could throw her arms around her brother. "I will never give up hope, Hunter. You did nothing wrong and I will do whatever it takes to prove that to the world."

Whatever brief moment of levity they had shared over the memory of a stray mutt, Hunter had once more donned that impassive mask. "Don't waste your life on me, Tay. I'm not worth it. Go back and finish your residency. Be a doctor. Help people."

She wanted that—oh, how she wanted that—but right now she had other work.

"I'll see you next Tuesday," she said.

He looked as if he wanted to argue, but the guard roughly snapped on the transfer handcuffs and led him out of the room.

She watched him go, his back tall and straight, and wondered how much more of him would crumble away before next Tuesday.

Wyatt never minded waiting.

He considered it research, a rare and wonderful chance to study people in a variety of situations, the whole rich texture of the human experience.

He spent the twenty minutes he waited for Taylor cataloguing the others in the waiting room, wondering about their stories, imagining the journeys their lives had taken to lead them to this point.

As he did wherever he went, his mind recorded impressions as he looked around the room.

He saw an older woman with stunning blue eyes and a face etched with character holding tight to the arms of her chair, her spine straight and her feet in their sensible brown shoes precisely lined up on the floor. Was she here to see a son or a grandson? he wondered.

Across the room sat a man of about fifty with a tattoo of an American flag just below his shirtsleeve and an Elvis-like pompadour and sideburns. He was a mechanic, Wyatt figured, at least judging by the grime under his fingernails and the faint shadow of permanent oil stains on the knees of his jeans. The man fidgeted and glanced at the clock every few moments while pretending to leaf through a hot-rod magazine.

Nearest the door to the visiting area sat a pregnant girl who couldn't have been a day older than eighteen, her belly stretched beneath a blue T-shirt that exposed a few inches of skin above her low-rider jeans. She chewed gum loudly and looked bored to tears, but every once in a while she paused to lay a loving hand across her stomach and her heavily made-up features would soften with a warm maternal glow.

No, he didn't mind waiting. This was life, gritty and real.

He was making a few notes from his conversation with Hunter in the steno notebook he had carried in with him when the man's sister walked through the checkpoint.

She wasn't a frail woman by any means, but for just a moment as she paused there at the entrance to the waiting room, she looked fragile, brittle almost. When she caught sight of him, he watched her take a deep breath and then paste on a polite smile as she walked toward him with a grace that seemed out of place here.

"Mr. McKinnon. Thank you for waiting."

She was extraordinarily beautiful, he thought, with that luminous skin and those dark blue eyes. He wondered if she had any idea how fresh and lovely she looked here in these grim surroundings, even with exhaustion stamped on her features.

"No problem. I didn't mind, especially since I cut into your time with your brother."

She looked as if she wanted to say something, then changed her mind.

"I wanted to apologize for the other night at your book signing, for coming on so strong," she said after a moment. "I suppose I'm a little too protective of Hunter. He tells me I am, anyway."

"It's natural in this situation. Perfectly understandable. You want to make everything right again for him, the way things were before all of this happened."

"I can't do that." The bleakness in her voice gave him the oddest urge to pull her into his arms.

"Probably not." He debated the wisdom of his next words, then threw caution to the wind. "Your brother knows his own mind. Despite the fact that most of his life is out of his control now and other people now tell him when he can shower and what he can eat, he's not helpless. He has his reasons for wanting to tell his story and he trusts me not to write a 'salacious' book. Maybe you should too."

She winced at his deliberate use of her word from the other night. "I'm sorry. I shouldn't have said that. I've read a few of your books and none of them were salacious. I'm sure this one wouldn't be either."

She closed her eyes for a moment and he was struck by the pale tracery of veins in her eyelids. She had the delicate skin of a redhead but she still looked as if she had spent too much time indoors lately.

When she opened her eyes again there was a determined light in them. "You're right, Hunter wants you to do this book and he's asked me to cooperate with you. I can do little enough to help him, but at least I can do this."

"Against your better instincts."

"Maybe. But haven't you ever gone ahead with something when your instincts were telling you to run, Mr. McKinnon?"

He thought of how his own instincts were warning him right now to run away from this woman with her expressive eyes and her passionate defense of her brother. If he let her, he had a strong feeling she could be hazardous not only to this project but, worse, to his heart.

"Listen, I know a great diner in Draper," he said, deciding to ignore his better judgment. "What do you say I buy you a cup of coffee and we can talk about the book? I'll see if I can allay some of your concerns—and maybe convince you to call me Wyatt."

Indecision flickered on her features. She started to nibble her lip, then checked the motion. "All right," she said, with a quick glance at her watch. "I have a study group at seven but I'm free until then."

Wyatt refused to worry about the excitement flowing through him at the idea of spending a few more minutes with Taylor Bradshaw.

Chapter 3

He beat her to the diner.

Despite the hour—too early for dinner, too late for lunch—several of the booths at Dewey's were full when Wyatt walked inside alone. The squat, unassuming restaurant served to-die-for mashed potatoes and several kinds of divine pie. It was a popular spot with visitors to the prison and with guards after their shifts.

He had always found it odd how much economic development seemed to spring up around prisons, the thriving little microeconomies correctional facilities fostered.

Taylor arrived just as the hostess was finding a booth for them. "Sorry," she said, somewhat breathlessly. "I wasn't paying attention and drove right past the place."

"No problem. You're here now."

They slid into opposite sides of the brown vinyl booth with the awkwardness of near-strangers suddenly finding themselves in close quarters. After a few moments of perusing the menu, Taylor ordered a chicken taco salad and a diet cola while he settled for coffee and a slice of Dewey's famous boysenberry pie.

"I didn't have time for lunch today," Taylor explained after the waitress walked away to give their order to the kitchen, "and my study group will probably go long past dinnertime. This might be my only chance to eat until midnight."

"What class is your study group for?"

She made a face. "Constitutional law. My least favorite class. I need all the help I can get in there."

"Why would a medical student need to study constitutional law?" he asked, genuinely baffled.

"A medical student wouldn't. It's a requirement for second-year law students, though."

He stared at her. "When did that happen? During the trial I could swear I heard you were attending the U. medical school, that you were close to graduation. I thought somebody told me you intended to specialize in pediatrics."

If he hadn't been watching her so closely, he might have missed the quick spasm of misery that crossed her features before they became impassive again.

"Things change."

"Wow. I'll say. Law school now? That's a major career shift."

She absently fiddled with a sugar packet from the wire rack on the table. "Sometimes you think you have your life all nicely mapped out. Then fate picks you up, shakes you around until your teeth rattle, and plops you down on a completely different path."

Try as he might, he couldn't picture her as an attorney, starchy suit and case files and law books. The whole white coat–stethoscope thing seemed a much better fit.

He wasn't sure why, he only knew that Dr. Taylor Bradshaw sounded much more natural to his ear than Taylor Bradshaw, Esquire.

"Why law?" he asked.

She paused for several seconds, her brow creased as if struggling to formulate an answer. She opened her mouth to respond, but before she could speak, the waitress arrived their order.

"Here you go, doll," the cheerful waitress said as she set Taylor's taco salad in front of her with a flourish.

In all the times he had been here, Wyatt had never seen the woman with anything but a smile on her face.

"Let me tell you, that chicken is delish today. It's always good but today the cook outdid himself. I had it for my own lunch and just about licked the plate clean."

She handed Wyatt his pie with a wink. "And I don't have to tell you how good the boysenberry pie is, since you order it just about every time you come in. Enjoy."

She had just left when a group of three men walked past. One of them paused and did a double take at their booth as Wyatt was enjoying his first sweet taste of berries.

"Taylor? What are you doing here?"

Wyatt chewed and swallowed while he tried to suppress his irritation at recognizing the balding man in the high-dollar suit. At first glance, Martin James looked mild-mannered and unprepossessing. He was about the same height as Taylor, slightly pudgy, with smooth, pleasant features and warm brown eyes.

First impressions could be deceiving, though. In this case, the man was a shark in the courtroom, one of the most sought-after defense attorneys in the state. But even James's reputation for dogged determination and creative representation hadn't been enough to acquit at least one of his infamous clients—Hunter Bradshaw.

Taylor apparently didn't hold a grudge at the man who had been unable to see her brother acquitted. She rose with delight on her features and kissed Martin James on his round cheek. "It's Tuesday. I always visit on Tuesday, remember? What about you? Have you been to see Hunter?"

"No. I had an appointment with one of my other clients," the attorney said. "If I had remembered Tuesdays were your day to visit, my dear, we could have driven out together."

She smiled at the man with a familiarity that surprised Wyatt, until he remembered hearing during the trial that Martin James and Taylor's late father, William Bradshaw, had been friends outside the courtroom.

"Thanks," she answered, "but I didn't feel much like being in a NASCAR time trial today."

"Are you insinuating I drive too fast?" Martin asked her with mock offense.

"Not at all. I think the fingernail gouges in my thighs have almost healed from the last time I rode somewhere with you."

Martin laughed and squeezed her hand.

As Wyatt watched, Taylor suddenly seemed to remember his presence.

"I'm sorry. Martin, this is Wyatt McKinnon."

"We've met," James said, all warmth gone from his voice and his features like a January cold snap. "McKinnon."

He nodded with the same coolness. Hunter Bradshaw wasn't the first client of Martin James whose story he had written. Wyatt's second book, *Eye of the Storm,* had chronicled the kidnap and murder of Rebecca Jordan. Martin James had represented Rebecca's husband, convicted of paying two teenagers to kill his wife. The attorney hadn't been at all thrilled to show up in *Eye of the Storm,* especially as Wyatt had chronicled some of the backdoor wrangling that had gone on between attorneys involved in the case.

James had threatened to sue him for defamation of character, but the threats never went anywhere, since Wyatt had documentation that every word in his book had been true.

Taylor looked from one to the other as if trying to figure out what had sparked the sudden tension. "Wyatt is writing a book about Hunter's case," she told the attorney. who looked not at all surprised—or pleased—by the information.

"I know. Your brother told me he was talking to him."

"Martin was a good friend of our father's and represented Hunter at trial," she explained to Wyatt, then winced. "I guess you would know that about the trial anyway. I forgot you were there. You would have seen him in the courtroom."

"Right. How are you, Martin?" Wyatt asked.

"Fine. Busy. I'm up to my ears in cases."

The affection on Taylor's features hardened a little and she sent the attorney a pointed look. "That must be why you haven't returned any of my calls or e-mails for the past two weeks."

A trapped light entered Martin's eyes and he suddenly looked as if he wanted to be somewhere else, somewhere far away. "I was out of town last week at a conference in Santa Barbara."

"What about this week?"

Though the cornered look was still there in his eyes, Martin's sigh was heavy and heartfelt. "I wish I had all the time in the world to devote to Hunter's appeal, but I don't. Your brother is not my only client, Taylor. You know that."

She didn't look appeased by his excuse. "How many of those other clients are fighting for their lives? Are any of the others on death row?" Her mouth tightened. "Are any of the others the son of one of your closest friends?"

Martin glared at her. "That's not fair."

Taylor drew in a breath, and Wyatt watched her visible attempts at calm.

"You're right, it's not," she murmured. "I'm sorry, Martin. I know you did your very best for Hunter during the trial. I'm just not ready to give up yet."

"Who said anything about giving up? I'm working up several briefs for his appeal and should be filing them anytime now."

"Did you get those citations I sent you? *People v. Loden* and *California v. Junger*?"

"Yes. I haven't had a chance to properly determine relevance but I'll put one of my associates on it right away, I promise."

"That's what you said with the last cites I sent you, and so far I haven't heard anything from you. Martin, I need your help. I can't do this by myself."

Martin brushed a hand over her hair in a gesture of both comfort and affection. "I know, shortcake. I'm sorry I haven't been able to give this my whole attention the past few months. I haven't forgotten Hunter's appeal—how could I? Let's meet next week for a strategy session and we can go over everything you've found. Does Monday night work for you?"

"I have a class that night. What about Tuesday?"

"Sounds good. Listen, I've got to run. Judy's got tickets to Ballet West tonight and I've got a dozen things to do before I can break away. She'll skin me alive if I'm late."

"Give her my love," Taylor said.

"You need to come for dinner sometime soon. I remember what being a second-year was like—you need to keep your strength up."

"I know. Thanks."

Martin kissed her cheek, gave Wyatt a curt nod, then hurried out of the diner, leaving the scent of some kind of smooth, undoubtedly expensive cologne behind him.

Wyatt stared after him, his mind processing the interaction between the lawyer and Taylor Bradshaw. Suddenly all the pieces clicked into place.

"That's why you switched to law school."

She paused in the middle of taking a sip of cola to blink at him. "Excuse me?"

"Hunter. You quit medical school so you can devote yourself to helping your brother appeal his conviction."

She set her glass down quickly as if it contained rat poison. For several long seconds she said nothing, then she faced him, her chin lifted—with determination or defiance, he wasn't sure.

"All the medical degrees in the world won't help me save my brother's life."

He wasn't sure why her sacrifice bothered him so much. Whatever she did wasn't any of his business—he barely knew the woman. She could decide to pitch a tent in the parking lot of the prison and his opinion wouldn't matter a whit. Still, for some reason it stung like a fresh blister that she had decided to give up her dream on such a hopeless quest.

"What do you think you're going to accomplish as a second-year law student that Martin James—one of the most successful litigators in the western United States—couldn't manage to do?"

"I don't know. But I have to try. I can't sit by and do nothing."

"What does Hunter think about this whole thing?"

She shrugged. "He's not happy about it, but he understands it's something I have to do. You have no idea what its like to feel completely powerless to help someone you love."

"Don't I?" he murmured, clearly seeing the image never far from the surface—of a sweet little curly-blond-haired girl disappearing in a puff of exhaust while her skinny, gawky older brother frantically dug through sunbaked grass for the broken shards of his glasses.

He thought of how both he and Gage had never given up hope of finding their little sister. They had worked relentlessly over the years, following cold leads, looking for patterns, trying to see inside the mind of the sort of person who might commit such a heinous act against an innocent child and her family.

In the twenty-three years since he had last seen Charlotte running through the sprinklers of their Las Vegas front yard, he had never stopped loving her, missing her, searching for her. He had never given up—nor would he—and he knew Gage felt the same.

He couldn't fault Taylor for her passionate effort to do anything necessary to appeal her brother's conviction. How could he, when he had spent more than two decades chasing the ghost of his little sister?

"I couldn't live with myself if I sat by and did nothing." Taylor continued. "Hunter is innocent. No matter how strong the state's case was against him, I will never believe otherwise."

He studied her in the bright fluorescent lights of the diner. "You believe it strongly enough to change the entire course of your life?"

"How could I possibly go out into the world and try to save the lives of strangers, knowing that I did absolutely nothing to save the life of my own brother?"

"Do you miss med school?"

To his chagrin, her smile looked a little wobbly. "Like crazy," she answered quietly, picking at her salad. "I've never wanted to be anything but a doctor, from the time I was a little girl. But I can always go back to med school once he's free again. Hunter is worth any sacrifice."

Wyatt couldn't help comparing her devoted relationship with her brother to his own relationship with Gage. His brother, three years older, was an FBI agent assigned to the Salt Lake field office. Until a few months earlier when their paths had intersected again, they had had a polite relationship but little more than that. In most respects, they were strangers.

Once Gage had been his hero. Wyatt had idolized his older brother and wanted nothing more than to be just like him. Gage had been well-liked, athletic, the epitome of cool to his awkward nerd of a kid brother.

Charlotte's kidnapping when he was nine and Gage twelve had changed everything. Each of them had retreated into a lonely world of remorse, regret. Guilt.

The strain and grief had been too much for their parents' marriage and Sam and Lynn McKinnon eventually split up a year after the kidnapping that had ripped apart their world.

In what Wyatt was sure they considered a fair and logical arrangement at the time, Gage had stayed with their father in Las Vegas while Wyatt had been forced to pack up his books and his chemistry set and return with Lynn to her family's ranch in Utah.

He had always felt that he had effectively lost not only a sister but a brother the day Charlotte was kidnapped.

He saw Gage only a handful of times during the rest of his childhood. His brother seemed to prefer things that way; their few encounters over the years had been marked by awkwardness and unease.

A few months after Gage moved back to Utah earlier in the summer, he was seriously injured during an attempt to arrest a suspect, and had met his fiancée Allie and her girls during his rehabilitation. In the process, Wyatt and his brother had begun to rebuild a relationship eroded over the years by time and distance.

He was rediscovering his brother, the strong, decent man he had admired so much during his early years, and he had to admit he was thoroughly enjoying the process.

He couldn't imagine how difficult it must be for Taylor to have her brother's pending execution hanging over her head.

"You called me quixotic," she said at his pensive silence. "You think I'm tilting at windmills here, don't you?"

He wanted to give her hope but he knew there was very little of that where Hunter Bradshaw was concerned. "You said it yourself. The case against your brother was a strong one, or twelve members of that jury wouldn't have voted unanimously, first for conviction, then for the death penalty. You face staggering odds against overturning his conviction."

Her eyes darkened with emotion at his words. "I know all that. But I have to try, Wyatt. I'm all he has."

Taylor heard the raw desperation in her voice and wanted to cringe. So much for coming off confident and assured. She sounded like a crazed zealot. Her goal was to convince Wyatt McKinnon she had evidence proving Hunter's innocence, not treat him to these maudlin displays of drama.

She had a fierce need for a little distance, and excused herself to hurry to the ladies' room.

Martin was partly to blame, she thought. His behavior today was nothing new. Since the trial he had been evasive and hedgy. Whenever she tried to work with him on the appeal, she was inevitably shuffled to some associate or other. It was like trying to nail down the breeze.

She knew the attorney had taken Hunter's conviction hard, had seen it as a personal failure. She didn't—she knew Martin had worked tirelessly to see Hunter acquitted. She just wished she could get the same effort out of him for the appeal.

In the small ladies' room, she gazed at herself in the round mirror and was horrified to see her coloring was blotchy and her eyes looked on the verge of tears. That was the problem with having auburn hair and pale skin—she could never hide her emotions. She blushed as easily as she could go deathly pale.

Out there in the diner she might have been only on the verge of tears, with not a single drop shed, but she still looked as if she'd been on a three-day crying jag.

Taylor spent several moments repairing her makeup and forcing herself to take slow, steady breaths until she felt once more in control, then returned to their booth.

She slid across from Wyatt. To her chagrin, she felt watery all over again at the look of concern on his lean features.

"I'm sorry. I'm not usually such an emotional wreck," she felt compelled to explain. "Visits to the prison are...difficult for me."

"I understand. I admire you for coming back week after week."

"I would say it gets easier but that would be a lie. I hated it as much today as I did the very first time I visited."

Taylor tried to swallow some of her salad, aware she didn't have much time before she would have to leave for her study group. "So when you interview family members of convicted murderers, what do you usually talk about?"

"Any insights they want to offer into why the crime happened. Some people blame it on difficult childhoods, others bring up failed relationships. It varies. I usually let the interviewee lead the conversation. If you talk to me, you can bring up anything you'd like that might help me understand your brother."

She could offer a hundred stories about how her brother had always protected her, how he had invariably stood between her and any threat, whatever the risk to himself. Telling any of them to Wyatt would be difficult, though, would expose dark family secrets she didn't like to even remember, let alone reveal to anyone else.

If she had to, she would tell him, though. Just not here. Not now.

"There is evidence that never came out in the trial, for various reasons," she said instead. "Evidence I believe proves his innocence beyond any reasonable doubt."

He looked intrigued. "What kind of evidence?"

"I have a whole room full of folders and a computer full of files. If I agree to talk to you for your book, give you whatever information you might be seeking about our family life or whatever, withholding nothing, will you at least look at what I have—*really* look at it—and judge his guilt or innocence for yourself?"

"Of course. Even if you don't want to be interviewed for the book I would still want to look at anything you have. Arriving at the truth is my ultimate goal as a writer. I wouldn't be any kind of researcher if I ignored important details that might help me get there."

Could it really be that easy? She hadn't even had to bargain with him—the curiosity in his eyes told her he meant what he said, that he would look at her collection of evidence without her having to bare any painful details of their childhood.

Relief swamped her like a warm, comforting tide. This could work. Kate's idea had been nothing less than inspired.

This man, with his clever mind and his insightful prose, could be a powerful ally.

Now all she had to do was hope that Wyatt could look at the evidence with an objective eye, untainted by the damning testimony offered during the trial.

She could always hope. She'd become an expert at that over the last thirty months.

Chapter 4

"You can't desert me, Kate," Taylor exclaimed. "This whole crazy thing was your idea!"

"Oh, no. Don't pin this one on me." Kate laughed. "I only suggested you talk to the man, try to get him on your side. The whole home-cooked dinner, wine and candlelight routine was completely your idea."

"I didn't cook anything! It's only takeout lasagna from La Trattoria. You think it's too much, don't you. It's too much. I knew it was. Okay, he won't be here for another half hour. I can just clear everything away, throw it all back in the fridge."

She reached for the place settings she had just spent ten minutes neurotically and meticulously arranging, but Kate grabbed her hands, laughter brimming in her blue eyes.

She squeezed her fingers. "Relax, Tay. I was only teasing you. Dinner is a great idea to soften him up. No man in his right mind can resist La Trat's lasagna."

Taylor pulled her hands free and let them fall to her side, mostly to keep from wringing them. "I'm not good at this stuff. You know I'm not."

"What stuff? I thought you were just meeting with the man to talk about Hunter's case."

Kate raised a knowing eyebrow and Taylor felt heat scorch her cheeks at her own transparency.

"We are. It's just…he's just…" She blew out a breath.

Kate grinned. "What? Too gorgeous for his own good?"

Her cheeks heated up a notch. "That too."

Kate's lighthearted teasing gave way to a worried expression. "You'll be careful, won't you?"

"Careful of what?"

"I haven't seen you like this about anyone since Rob. I just don't want you to be hurt again."

Taylor rearranged the place settings again, refusing to meet Kate's all-too-knowing gaze. "The situations aren't at all the same. Rob was a complete jerk."

"A jerk you were seriously thinking about marrying."

"In one of my more idiotic moments. Good thing I found out how shallow and ambitious he was in time, right? At the first sign of trouble he decided the woman he claimed to be passionately in love with wasn't nearly as important as his future political aspirations."

Hours after Hunter was arrested, when Taylor was been reeling from shock and disbelief, Rob Llewelyn had dumped her. He had his whole life mapped out, he had informed her with a self-righteousness that still made her burn at her own foolishness. First the state legislature, then a congressional seat, and after that, the sky was the limit.

Someone in his position had to be above reproach. He couldn't afford this kind of negative guilt by association, he told her. This was already shaping up to be a huge scandal and he couldn't have even a whiff of it tainting his future.

"Rob didn't hurt me," she said automatically, as she always did. "I had a lucky escape."

Though she believed the second part of her statement, the first part wasn't strictly true, she had to admit. Kate knew it too. Taylor might not have been sure she loved the man—in retrospect, she couldn't believe she had ever even entertained it as a possibility—but being dumped at such a traumatic time when she could have used all the support she could find had been one more shock to get over.

"Anyway, even if I am…attracted…to Wyatt McKinnon, I could never do anything about it. I don't have the time or energy for that kind of complication right now. I just don't. With school and Hunter and the appeal, I don't have anything left to give."

"Sometimes you just *have* to find the time and energy, especially when it comes to a man like McKinnon."

"Says the woman whose personal relationship rule is not to date the same man more than three times."

Kate gave her a pointed look. "Don't change the subject. We were talking about you, not me."

"I'd rather talk about you," Taylor muttered.

"I'm sure you would," Kate said. Her smile slid away after a moment. "I'm just saying be careful, that's all."

Obviously Taylor hadn't been as successful as she'd hoped at hiding from her friend the strange effect Wyatt had on her, if Kate thought this little lecture was necessary.

She had spent the past three days trying to figure out what it was about him that struck such a responsive chord in her. He was gorgeous, Kate was certainly right about that. Lean and masculine, with those intense eyes and his surprisingly sweet smile.

She suspected her strong reaction to him—and the disquiet it sparked in her—was from more than just a hormonal reaction to a gorgeous man. The other day at the diner, she had seen the kindness in his eyes. Something about his quiet calm had comforted her, steadied her, more than all the warm tea in the world.

"I'll be fine," she finally answered Kate, wishing she believed her own words. "I'd be better if I knew I could count on you for moral support. A nice, friendly buffer. I never would have brought home La Trattoria if I thought for one moment you would be abandoning me."

"Ha. Nice try. Your guilt trip is not going to work on me this time."

"Not even a little?" Taylor asked hopefully.

"I have rounds! I don't have any choice—I can't help it if my schedule was changed. With this flu outbreak, Sterling has all the residents on double shifts. I'm going to be late as it is if I don't hurry!"

Taylor gave her a quick hug. "Don't worry about me. I'm sorry I badgered you."

Kate hurried for the front door to pick up the battered denim jacket she adored. She grabbed her keys off the hall table. "You know I'm going to expect total deets in the morning, right? I'll pick up Krispy Kreme on my way home, so be ready to spill."

"I will." Taylor gave her another hug. "You can have leftover lasagna and doughnuts for breakfast."

"Mmm. My favorite."

With a laugh, Kate rushed out the door. Taylor watched her go, aware of the jealousy settling like a hard, greasy lump in her stomach.

She wanted to be the one running out the door to the hospital. Just went to show how crazy she was, she thought, that she could actually envy Kate the upcoming twelve hours on her feet dealing with surly patients and reams of paperwork.

She fiercely wanted to go back and finish medical school, to serve the residency she'd been promised in pediatrics. She had told Wyatt the truth about that the other day at the diner. Though she knew it wasn't fair, that it was petty and small, sometimes it chewed her up inside that Kate had the freedom to follow her dreams while Taylor was trapped in a world she hated, a world that threatened to suck the life out of her.

Taylor sighed, ashamed of her moment of weakness. How could she feel sorry for herself and decry her own lack of freedom? If the mood struck her, she could walk outside right now and enjoy the cool bite of an October evening or the sweet scent of the late-blooming flowers in her garden.

She could run to her favorite Italian restaurant for all the lasagna her heart desired, could top it off with a big bowl of triple chocolate Häagen-Dazs from the freezer if she wanted.

Hunter could do none of those things. He truly had no freedom, no choices. Until he did, she could put her own dreams on hold.

Wyatt wasn't sure what to expect from Taylor's house. From his research and from testimony during the trial, he knew she came from money—her great-grandfather Bradshaw had been a wealthy silver baron in Park City during its mining heyday. Through prudent investments, the Bradshaws had managed to hang on to their money at a time when many other mining magnates went broke.

That had been one of the more intriguing aspects of her brother's case that the media had played up relentlessly—Hunter had come from wealth and privilege. He hadn't needed to work a day in his life if he didn't want to, yet he had dirtied his hands by playing at being a cop. Rich boy turned cop turned killer.

For all he knew, Taylor could live in some starchy Avenues mansion. But when he followed the directions she'd given him three days earlier, he found a neighborhood of small cottages. Though the houses were small and the yards minuscule, this was a desirable area, neatly sandwiched between the University of Utah campus and Salt Lake City's downtown. The houses were old but charming, with residents who kept them freshly painted and tidy.

With its cheerful blue shutters and fall flower garden, Taylor's house reminded him a little of the cottage his brother Gage had rented in Park City earlier in the summer, where he had met his fiancée Allie and her two darling little girls.

A group of children played basketball on a standard tacked to the garage of the house next door, and on the other side, a rail-thin gray-haired man paused his leaf-raking long enough to study Wyatt with curiosity, making him wonder if Taylor didn't have many male callers.

Before he turned off his engine in front of her house, he saw a small silver Honda back out and drive away, but from his angle he couldn't get a glimpse of the driver.

Maybe Taylor chickened out and decided not to meet with him. Wyatt rejected the thought as soon as it entered his mind. She struck him as the kind of woman who would never back down from a fight. Besides, he had seen her car the other afternoon at the prison and knew she drove a Subaru wagon.

Anticipation flickered through him at knowing he would see her again. He was grimly aware that he had done entirely too much thinking about Taylor the past few days.

Objectivity.

He repeated the word in a low mantra as he hit the locks on his Tahoe and climbed out into the October evening. He might be fiercely attracted to Taylor, but he couldn't allow that to distract him from his goal. He was going to write her brother's story.

No, he corrected himself. He was going to write Dru and Mickie Ferrin's stories. Big difference, one he needed to remember. They were the reason he was here.

Taylor Bradshaw was a source for his book, that's all. As a loving, devoted sister, she could give him rare insight into her brother's mind and heart, perceptions he might not even be able to get from Bradshaw himself. She could tell him what it had been like growing up as the two children of a man who by all accounts had been as strict with his children as he'd been on the bench.

Maybe she could even shed some light into what might have made Hunter snap that night.

He rang the doorbell and smiled at the curious neighbor, amused that the elderly man was still watching with his rake in his hands as if he was prepared to use it if Wyatt threatened Taylor in any way.

The door opened a moment later and, before he could even say hello, he was accosted by a sleek Irish setter. The dog didn't bark at him or jump up, but she blocked his way inside, sniffing and wagging her tail in greeting, until he reached down to pet her.

She immediately took that as permission to get up close and personal. She rubbed her head against his thigh eagerly, that long auburn tail going like crazy.

Taylor stepped forward, her color high—at the dog's friendliness or at something else, he couldn't begin to guess. "Belle, leave the poor man alone. Down," she ordered. The dog whined a little but obeyed, slinking down to the tile floor.

"Sorry about that. I'm afraid Belle is a cheap hussy for any man who gives her a little attention," she said. "Most women she can take or leave, but whenever a man comes to the house, she is practically giddy. She misses Hunter, I think."

"She was his?"

Taylor nodded. "He raised her from a puppy. Actually, he rescued her from a crime scene. Belle's mother was shot trying to protect her owner from the woman's abusive boyfriend. Neither the dog nor the woman survived. There were three others in the litter, and Hunter and John Randall, his partner, made it their mission in life to find homes for all of them. He fell hard for Belle and couldn't give her up."

He tried—and failed—to imagine the tough man he met in prison rescuing a litter of orphaned puppies. With that hard, steely gaze of his, Wyatt had a difficult time imagining Hunter had a soft spot for much. Except maybe his sister.

"I guess you inherited her after his arrest."

"I'm just watching her until Hunter gets out," she said, her chin lifted defiantly as if daring him to contradict her.

Wyatt wasn't sure what to say to that, and they stood awkwardly in her small foyer for a few moments until she seemed to collect herself.

"I'm sorry, let me take your jacket."

He shrugged out of it and handed it to her. "Have you eaten?" she asked after she hung it in the closet off the entryway.

"No. I was going to ask if you wanted to grab something after we were done," he said. He didn't want to admit, even to himself, how much he had wanted her to agree.

"Do you like Italian?" she asked. "I picked up some takeout on the way home."

"Italian's great. If my mother were here, she'd tell you I never met a pasta dish I didn't like."

She looked vaguely surprised at his mention of his mother, as if she'd never given the matter of his parentage much thought. "Does your family live in Salt Lake?" she asked as she led the way through the small house toward the kitchen.

"We're all over. My parents split up when I was a kid. Mom lives in Liberty near my ranch—she's an elementary school principal—and my dad has a carpentry shop in Las Vegas. I have an older brother who has lived all over the West but currently hangs his hat in Park City. He's with the FBI."

"FBI? Really? So I guess you both work closely with criminals."

He sent her an amused look. "Something like that."

The kitchen reminded him of a Tuscan farmhouse, with warm yellow stuccoed walls and pots hanging from a center island. It looked comfortable and well-used. He leaned a hip against the counter as he watched her transfer a pan from the oven to a dining table set in a small alcove overlooking her backyard.

"So your parents had just two boys?" she asked, her hands too busy with setting out food to notice the reaction he knew he wouldn't be able to hide at her innocent question.

He thought of Charlotte—little Charley—with her blond curls and her sweet smile. Guilt socked him in the gut, as it always did. "We had a little sister but we lost her when she was three."

It was his easy, glib answer, the one he used when he didn't want to get into the whole story. He knew she would assume Charlotte died. Most people did. It was often easier to let them think that than going into all the grim details of the kidnapping, which would inevitably dominate the conversation for some time.

"Oh. I'm so sorry." Compassion turned her eyes a dewy midnight blue and filled him with guilt at his lie of omission.

He chose to deal with it by changing the subject quickly. "Everything looks delicious. This is great. You didn't have to go to so much trouble."

"I didn't do anything but pick up the lasagna from a restaurant. I wish I could say I made it, but Kate—my roommate—is the expert in the kitchen. I'm learning from her but I still am an amateur. I thought she would be here to join us but her shift was changed at the hospital. You just missed her."

Did she tell him that to subtly remind him this wasn't a date? he wondered. That even though they were two adults enjoying a delicious meal alone together, he shouldn't make any kind of leap in logic about it?

Too bad the roommate wasn't here. There was an intimacy to being alone together here that he would have preferred to avoid, given his attraction to her.

Objectivity, he reminded himself as he poured wine for both of them. This was just another interview, just like dozens of others he'd done for this book.

This wasn't so bad, Taylor thought a few moments later as she took another bit of rich, spicy lasagna.

All her nervousness had been for nothing. Wyatt seemed to find nothing odd about sharing a meal before they got down to the gritty business of going over the facts in Hunter's case. As they enjoyed the delectable pasta and crusty Italian bread, they talked of mundane matters—her classes, his ranch, how long she'd lived in the house.

"I bought it after my father died four years ago."

"Your mother died when you were just a little girl. Six, isn't that right?"

The question was a blunt reminder of the unpalatable fact that he knew far more about her than she did about him. She couldn't help feeling a little exposed that so many private details of her life had become public knowledge after Hunter's arrest. Her sense of invasion made her reply sharper than she had intended.

"And I guess that's the explanation you're going to use for everything that supposedly went wrong with Hunter."

He looked surprised by the sudden attack, then thoughtful. "No. I was just thinking how tough that must have been on you, losing a mother at such an early age."

The age hadn't been as difficult as the circumstances of her mother's death. "My mother was…ill for a long time before she died. I don't remember her any other way."

She didn't add that Angela Bradshaw had suffered from a grab bag of mental health issues or that few of the snippets of memory she had of her mother were pleasant.

"What was Hunter like as a big brother?"

She gave him a cool look over the lip of her wineglass. "Is this on the record?"

"Up to you."

She debated exactly what to tell him as the spectres of those dark family secrets loomed. For so much of her life, she had tried to pretend those first six years didn't exist, that they were just some murky nightmare.

She didn't like remembering how bad things had been as Angela's condition deteriorated. She didn't talk about it with anyone—choosing to break her silence to someone writing a book didn't seem the greatest idea.

On the other hand, her ultimate goal was to convince Wyatt that Hunter wasn't capable of murdering anyone. To do that, she would have to tell him at least something of their childhood.

"He was older than me by five years. I guess you know that."

"So that makes you twenty-six."

"Right. Five years doesn't seem like much when you're thirty-one and twenty-six, but take away a few decades and it's a huge chasm at eleven and six. I think most boys that age would rather be caught in their Underoos on the school playground than be seen hanging around with their little sisters, but Hunter never seemed to mind me tagging after him. He was a great brother and never treated me with anything but love and kindness. I don't remember him ever yelling at me or teasing me. He looked out for me. Protected me."

He frowned at this. "Against what?"

She should tell him now. This was the perfect opportunity. The words hovered inside her, but in the end she chickened out. Once he knew the truth about Angela, he would jump to more wrong conclusions about Hunter—and about her.

"He protected me against anything that threatened me," she said instead. "I love him and I know him, probably better than anyone else in the world. He can be a tough man when it's necessary. A hard one. He has a strong sense of justice and maybe sees things as too black or white, but no matter what the provocation, he would never murder anyone. The man I know—the man I grew up in the same house with, simply isn't capable of it."

"Nice opening statement, Counselor."

Her smile was small and rueful. "Sorry. I guess I tend to come off a little strong. I probably sound like a zealot."

"You sound like a loving sister trying to help her brother."

Trying, maybe, but for all her efforts, she didn't seem to have been accomplishing much. Spinning her wheels, that's all she seemed to be doing since his conviction.

They had finished eating, she saw, and though under other circumstances she would have enjoyed lingering around the table and learning more about him, she knew she couldn't afford to waste his time. "I have tiramisu. If you'd like, we can have coffee with it in my office while I show you the evidence I've collected since the trial."

"Sounds great."

She loved her small office, filled with comfortable, favorite pieces of furniture she had moved here from her father's library after his death when she and Hunter sold the house on Walker Lane. No surprise, Hunter hadn't wanted any of it. As far back as she could remember, he and the Judge had a stormy relationship and she was fairly certain Hunter had few pleasant memories of the oak-paneled room where their father had presided with such a firm hand.

She found it peaceful, though. This was where she worked, where she preferred to study. She and Kate had crammed for many med school exams behind this desk. It had always been a refuge from the stress of life.

But when she walked inside with Wyatt behind her, the room seemed to shrink. He had such a commanding presence, a masculine confidence she found entirely too attractive.

Wyatt took the burgundy leather armchair opposite her desk, stretched out his long legs, and watched her expectantly.

Taylor didn't quite know where to start. She had volumes of information carefully organized—court transcripts, the police report, newspaper clippings, eyewitness reports. She had more files on her computer, information she regularly dumped to her laptop.

What would he find most compelling? she wondered.

"You were in the courtroom so you know the basics of the case," she began.

"I wasn't there every day," he answered, "but I have studied the court transcript extensively."

Sitting behind the desk with him on the other side seemed

entirely too formal, so she chose to perch on the edge, trying not to fidget. "Then you know the state's case against Hunter was completely circumstantial. They had nothing to prove beyond a reasonable doubt that Hunter killed Dru or Mickie."

"It was circumstantial but it was strong. His fingerprints were all over the scene."

"He dated Dru for eighteen months. It would have been more unusual if his fingerprints weren't there! Don't you find it significant that they weren't on the murder weapon?"

"You mean the murder weapon that just happened to be registered to your brother?"

"Anyone could have fired that gun! He gave it to Dru the week before the murders, for protection after she received death threats."

Wyatt frowned. "So he says. No one could substantiate either the death threats or your brother's claim that he gave her his weapon. If she was threatened, she didn't tell anyone else but your brother."

As it always did when she heard the evidence against her brother, Taylor's blood pressure seemed to rise. She wanted to snap back an angry retort, but that wouldn't accomplish her goal. She was supposed to be showing him new facts, convincing him of Hunter's evidence, not rehashing all the damning evidence from the trial.

"My brother was an experienced detective," she said after a moment of deep breathing for calm. "Don't you think if he was going to kill someone with his own weapon he would certainly be smart enough not to leave it behind for the whole world to find?"

She didn't give him time to respond. "And let's focus on the weapon. It was wiped clean, right? But the state crime lab did retrieve one partial from the safety. Did you know that?"

He frowned, his expression puzzled. "I don't believe I remember hearing that."

"You didn't know because it never came out at trial," she answered. "I only found out myself after Hunter's conviction, when I was contacted by the crime lab technician who couldn't figure out why her report about the fingerprint—that didn't belong to Hunter or to Dru or Mickie—wasn't used by the defense."

"Good question. Why wasn't it?"

"Because we didn't know about it! It was never included in discovery, and now the entire report and photographs of the partial seem to have disappeared, the hard copies and the computer files."

"Is that the basis for your appeal?"

"One of them. That and the eyewitness who said she saw a late-model luxury sedan leaving the scene right after she heard gunshots. Hunter drives a Jeep Cherokee that just happened to be parked at the Doughnut Falls trailhead, thirty miles away, at the time of the shooting, according to other eyewitnesses."

Wyatt sat forward, his puzzled frown deepening. "Is the eyewitness who saw a vehicle leaving the scene something else the defense didn't know?"

Taylor curled a hand against her thigh. "No. Martin knew about Mrs. Hancey. But she's seventy-five years old and she had been drinking that night. He didn't think she would make a strong witness."

"But you believe her?"

"Yes! She has no doubt whatsoever about what she saw. Someone else was there that night, Wyatt. I know that with all my heart, just as I know that when I find out who it was, I will find whoever killed Dru and Mickie."

Chapter 5

After her impassioned declaration, Wyatt studied Taylor Bradshaw.

The recessed can lighting overhead and rich colors in the small office picked up golden highlights in her auburn hair and turned her eyes a vivid blue. He couldn't look away, not from the allure of her features and not from the fervent conviction in her voice.

Objectivity.

The concept suddenly seemed harder than he had ever imagined. How was he supposed to keep things polite and impersonal between them with this attraction seething inside his skin? He wanted fiercely to kiss her, to direct that passion to something other than her fight to save her brother.

What the hell was wrong with him? This instant heat churning through his blood whenever he was around Taylor

Bradshaw was an entirely new experience. He enjoyed women and dated a wide variety, but he was far from a womanizer.

Something about Taylor was different. He remembered the first time he had seen her, looking pale and frightened in the courtroom during Hunter's first court appearance. Even then—when he had no idea who she was, only that she obviously had some connection to the defendant—he had been overwhelmed by a powerful desire to protect her, to help her, to ease that fear in her eyes.

He didn't understand it then and he sure didn't understand it now. He only knew he had never reacted this way to a woman. He wasn't at all the sort of man tempted to steal kisses from a woman he barely knew—especially one with such a tangle of complications.

While they were not exactly adversaries, they were certainly coming at this case from different directions. She fiercely believed in her brother's innocence while Wyatt had sat through the trial convinced just as staunchly that Hunter deserved the sentence he received.

Intellectually he knew Hunter was guilty. As he had said to her, the state's case had been a strong one, if circumstantial. But listening to the conviction in her voice, to her passionate defense of her brother, it was hard not be swayed.

The urge to step forward, slide her down from that big desk and into his arms, was almost more than he could fight down, but he gave it his best effort.

He had no business touching her, not when he was writing a book about her brother's case. If he thought their relationship was a tangled one now, how much more snarled would it become if he kissed her?

This book was too important to him to risk screwing it up because of some strange reaction to a woman he barely knew.

Wyatt blew out a breath, compelled to do something to put distance between them—in his own mind, if nothing else.

"I went to school with Dru Ferrin."

At his blunt pronouncement, she stared at him, her eyes an impossible blue. "You did?"

"Yes. She was a friend. A good one at a time when I didn't have very many others. She was the first girl I ever kissed, clear back in the second grade, before my family moved away. When I came back, she was always kind to me."

"I see." She looked down at the notes in front of her, neatly typed and organized. When she met his gaze again, her expression was cool, almost resigned. "That's why you've chosen this case to write about."

He nodded. "I knew as soon as I heard about the murders that I had to write this one, long before I knew any details of the case or anything about your brother. I *have* to. I owe it to an old friend."

She said nothing for several moments, the only sound in the office the buzz of the computer behind her. Finally she met his gaze, and Wyatt regretted to see the fire in those eyes had faded to bleak resignation.

"So you already have your mind made up that Hunter is guilty. Nothing I say, no evidence I show you, will change that, will it."

"I didn't say that. I want to write about what really happened to Dru and her mother." Wyatt chose his words carefully. "If Hunter didn't kill them, I certainly want to find whoever did as much as you do. But I wanted you to know where I'm coming from. I'm on Dru's side here. I don't have any other choice."

"I read the article about you in *Vanity Fair*. You write for 'the victims and the victims' families.' That's what you said."

He winced. That article had been a huge mistake from start to finish. He usually shied away from that kind of publicity, but his agent and publisher had pushed him to agree to this one to promote his new book.

At the time Wyatt thought the tradeoff they were agreeing to would be worth it—in exchange for him agreeing to the *Vanity Fair* thing, they would cut the six-week book tour they were pushing to two, with a few scattered media appearance here and there.

He didn't like the limelight, but he had accepted after the overwhelming public response to his first book—and to each subsequent one—that it was the steep price he had to pay for success.

The quote Taylor recited about his reasons for writing hadn't been the full truth. He hadn't told the *Vanity Fair* reporter about Charlotte and the reporter hadn't managed to dig up that information, despite it being public record.

His little sister was the real reason for everything he wrote. Somehow, by writing about other victims, other crimes, he hoped to gain a kind of understanding into why she was taken.

So far it had eluded him, but he knew that with each book he came closer to the one he would someday have to write about his own family's ordeal.

"It's not an easy thing for a family who has lost someone they care about to open up to someone who's going to write about their case," he answered finally. "I hope I've treated the stories of every crime victim I've written about with dignity and respect. I just thought you ought to know I had a personal connection to Dru."

"Thank you for telling me," Taylor said quietly. "While we're being honest with each other, I should tell you that I never liked Dru. My brother was crazy about her and wanted us to be friends. I tried, I really did, but all I could see was the way she manipulated him. I thought she was destructive and ambitious. I was never sure if she was really interested in him or just using him as an inside source at the police station. When he found out she was pregnant, he insisted they marry and do right by the child, but Dru refused over and over again."

"The baby wasn't his, though."

Her expression twisted with bitterness and she rose from the desk and stalked to the window. "Right. But Dru never murmured a word that the baby's paternity might be in question to Hunter. I don't know, maybe she didn't know herself who the father was. Maybe she didn't want to marry Hunter until she knew for sure, but as far as my brother knew, he had fathered a child whose mother refused to marry him. It ate him up inside."

"The state claimed he found out the baby wasn't his and that's why he killed her, in a jealous rage."

"That was a lie! Absolutely ridiculous. I don't believe he had any clue she was seeing anyone else—I was with him when he received the DNA report after the autopsy, proving the baby wasn't his. I saw how shell-shocked the news made him."

When he didn't respond, she continued, her voice becoming more impassioned as she went. "Do you understand what I'm telling you? As you said, the prosecution used that as his motive for killing her—Hunter supposedly flew into a jealous rage after he found out she was pregnant with another man's child. Their theory is that he confronted her about it that night, took his gun along with him for good measure, and ended up shooting her and Mickie."

"Right."

"It didn't happen, Wyatt! He didn't even know until two

days after she died about the results of the DNA tests. I was with him! I know without any doubt whatsoever in my mind that before that moment he received that report, he had no idea—*none*—that the baby wasn't his. Think about it. How would you feel after you had just spent two days grieving for your child and the woman you loved, to be confronted with undeniable evidence that child wasn't yours after all?"

Taylor didn't give him a chance to answer. "I saw his face, the total sense of betrayal on it. He was stunned. So explain to me how jealousy could be his motive for killing them if he didn't even know she had been sleeping with someone else until two days after the murders?"

There was a damn good question, one he was surprised hadn't been presented by the defense. On the other hand, Taylor was the defendant's sister. She had already proved by her actions since Hunter's conviction that she was fiercely loyal and protective of her brother, that she would do anything to see him cleared of the charge against him.

Her credibility was bound to be put into question by the prosecution, and maybe that was a risk Martin James hadn't been willing to take.

Still, it certainly raised questions. What if Taylor was right? What if the state's case against Hunter was nothing more than a flimsy house of cards? Take away the man's motive and the whole thing would blow away in a stiff breeze.

Dru deserved justice. That had been his goal in writing the book from the beginning—but he recognized that justice wouldn't be served by punishing an innocent man for her murder.

"The best way—really the only way—to prove your brother didn't kill Dru and her mother, Mickie, is to prove beyond any doubt that someone else did."

She nodded. "That's the direction I've been trying to go. I've made a list of possible suspects in the case—not specific people or anything, since I haven't been able to nail down any names, just profiles."

She dug through a pile of folders until she found the one she wanted. She handed it to him and Wyatt read it quickly. The list of people with motive to kill Dru Ferrin was a long one.

"Even though, as you said, no one else can substantiate them, I believe Hunter when he said Dru received death threats before she died. That's why he gave her his weapon, for protection. If I can find out who made those threats, that's a logical starting place. And the baby's real father is another possibility, if I could ever discover who else she might have been seeing. Also, Dru covered crime for the television station where she worked. Maybe she was working on a story someone didn't want her to report. Those are all possibilities."

Wyatt drew in a sharp breath, terribly afraid he would live to regret the ramifications of his next statement—and hoping like hell he knew what he was doing. "It looks like we've got a lot of work ahead of us, then," he said.

If he wanted to knock the pins clean out from under her, he had picked exactly the right words. She stared at him, her eyes wide and incredulous, as if she couldn't quite believe he meant his words—that he was even willing to entertain the possibility that Hunter might be innocent, or that he would consider helping her prove it.

"We?" she asked warily.

Wyatt shrugged. "I want justice for Dru and Mickie. If your brother didn't kill them—and I'll tell you up front I'm still not convinced of that—I want to know who did."

Gradually, the suspicion in her eyes gave way to a dawning excitement. Her expression relaxed, brightened. As the shadows lifted, she gave him what he suddenly realized was the first genuine smile he had ever seen on her face.

The impact of that smile plowed into him like a fist to the gut. It made her look young, so extraordinarily lovely and vibrant that his eyes almost hurt looking at her. He wanted to sit right here and bask in that smile, to do everything he could think of to make sure it stayed right there.

"Oh, Wyatt," she exclaimed. "Thank you!"

She reached for his hand to give it a grateful squeeze. At the contrast of her warm, soft skin against his, his blood thrummed in his ears and the fierce attraction he had spent the past hour battling surged up again.

"Don't thank me until we have something concrete," he answered gruffly. He tried to extricate his hand from hers but somehow he only succeeding in tugging her closer.

Objectivity.

He closed his eyes so he didn't have to watch the whole damn concept fly out the window. How could any man resist those dewy blue eyes, that smile that sent off enough wattage to light the whole valley?

When he opened his eyes, she was still staring at him as if he'd just lit the stars. He groaned and pulled her to him, his mind only consumed with tasting that smile.

He wanted to think he might have been able to keep the kiss light, just one small, seductive sample of her mouth that tasted of tiramisu.

But at the first touch of his lips, she sighed a what-took-you-so-long kind of sigh and melted in his arms, as if she'd been waiting for just this moment.

In his arms, Taylor felt as if she'd just walked out into bright sunshine after months in a dark, dank cave of uncertainty. She wanted to lift her face to that sunshine, to bask in it, to soak it into her skin.

For two and a half years she had lived with gnawing, relentless fear and a terrible burden of helplessness. But now Wyatt had agreed to look for answers with her and she almost couldn't believe how giddy she was at being able to share some of the weight of that load at last.

Her arms slipped around his neck and she leaned against him, drawn by his heat and strength. With a low sound of arousal, he deepened the kiss, pressing against her until her hips rested on the edge of the desk.

She wanted to absorb the leashed power she sensed in his muscles. Since the first time she saw him, she had found his lean, rangy build wildly sexy but she had never dreamed it would feel so right to be in his arms like this.

Taylor wasn't sure how long they kissed, she only knew it was slow and seductive and that for the first time in forever she forgot about the stress always waiting for her outside this room.

If she had her way, she would have stayed right here in this unexpected haven for at least another hour or two, but Belle's concerned whine from the doorway pierced the soft haze of desire surrounding her.

She blinked back to awareness, stunned at how quickly and easily she had become tangled around him.

Belle whined again. The setter had never seen her in this kind of situation, Taylor realized. She probably wasn't sure whether she ought to be protecting Taylor in some way.

If only the dog had come in a few minutes earlier, Taylor thought with a grimace, Belle might have prevented her from discovering just how attracted she was to Wyatt McKinnon.

She stepped away from him, embarrassed that she suddenly couldn't seem to catch her breath. She tried to remind her lungs to breathe, her heart to pulse again.

After giving Belle a shaky smile that seemed to reassure her, Taylor turned back to Wyatt.

"That was…unexpected."

"Right." He cleared his throat, his expression adorably baffled, as if he couldn't quite believe what had just happened between them. "Um, I don't want you to think I make a habit of that kind of thing."

"I don't. Think that, I mean. Or make a habit of that kind of thing myself, really."

"Okay, then."

They stood in awkward silence as Taylor frantically searched her mind for something to say. How was she supposed to make her brain work when all she wanted to do was melt into a gooey pile all over the carpet?

"Do you mean it, about helping me find who really killed Dru and Mickie?" she finally asked.

She found it strangely comforting that he seemed as disconcerted by the sudden heat between them as she was, and it took him several moments to answer. "I can't make any promises that what we find will change my opinion about who committed the murders, Taylor. But I'll do what I can to help you. I couldn't in good conscience write the book without thoroughly researching those angles you talked about."

Her heart sagged with relief and gratitude, and she would have kissed him again if she wasn't afraid where they might end up.

"I have an appointment Monday to talk to a reporter at the television station who was friends with Dru. You are welcome to come along if you'd like."

"What do you hope to find out from her?"

"I thought Dru might have told her what she was working on or about the threats she received or even given her some clue as to who might have fathered her baby."

"You don't think the police went over this with her?"

Usually she couldn't stop thinking about it, but for the first time in two and a half years she found it hard to concentrate on Hunter's case. She gave it her best shot, though. "I think the police found an obvious suspect in Hunter and decided to run with it, instead of exploring all of the possibilities."

"Even though Hunter was one of their own? I find that doubtful. Cops look out for each other."

That was one of the facts of the case that had convicted Hunter, she thought, in the court of public opinion anyway. Most people made the same assumption, that the police department would never have turned on one of their own unless the evidence against him was overwhelming and they had no choice.

"Hunter wasn't the most popular detective in the department," she said. "He didn't like some of the political games his superiors played and wasn't shy about making his views known. He was also involved, though peripherally, in a case that involved police misconduct, and he went to internal affairs about it. Some factions in the department considered him a traitor because of that and were only too willing to ignore any evidence that pointed to his innocence."

"I find it a little hard to believe the entire police department—not to mention the district attorney's office—conspired to convict an innocent cop just because he didn't win popularity contests."

Taylor managed to swallow her instinctive retort. He had said he would help her. That's all she could ask. If it meant facing his inherent skepticism, she would just meet every one of his doubts with evidence supporting Hunter's version of the facts.

And try to ignore the low heat of desire still rippling through her.

"Hey, Mister Wyatt, can I ride one of your horsies?"

Wyatt laughed down at the little moppet with the curly dark hair currently tugging on his jeans. Gabriella, one of his brother Gage's stepdaughters-to-be, looked up at him with liquid brown eyes, her cupid's bow of a mouth set in an eager, pleading smile.

Gage would need one heck of a hard heart to ever say no to this one, Wyatt thought. He could see it now—she and her younger sister would have his big tough FBI agent of a brother wrapped around her finger in a heartbeat.

He, of course, was made of sterner stuff.

"I've got just the pony for you, perfect for two little girls. You and Anna can both take turns riding her around the corral after lunch, but only if your mother says it's all right."

Gaby's attention shifted to his right. "Please, Mama. Can we please? Mister Wyatt says it's okay!"

With a wince, Wyatt turned to find Gage's fiancée approaching. Alicia DeBarillas planted her hands on her hips, but he caught the teasing glint in her eyes. "Thanks for backing me into a corner. How am I supposed to say no to a ride on a perfect pony?"

He grinned back at her. "You're not. That's the idea. There's nothing to worry about, I swear. Lucy is a very gentle pony and I promise I'll lead them around the corral the entire time."

"Please, Mama," Gaby repeated, turning the whole potent force of her persuasive pout in her mother's direction. "Pretty pretty please with ice cream on top?"

Allie appeared to think this over. "Is it chocolate-chunk ice cream with walnuts?"

Gaby giggled. "Nope. Strawberry."

"Ooh. My second favorite. Okay. As long as you listen carefully to whatever Wyatt tells you to do."

"Wahoo!" Gaby shrieked with excitement. "Wait until I tell Anna we're gonna ride one of Mister Wyatt's horsies!"

She started to rush off but Wyatt called her back. "Wait. You can only ride my pony on one condition. Since your mom is marrying my brother next week, that makes us family now. No more of this 'Mister' stuff, okay?"

She appeared to think this over. "Can I call you Uncle Wyatt? My friend Jessica has four uncles and I don't even have one! I don't think that's fair."

Wyatt blinked, a little nonplussed by the concept. "Sure. I've never been an uncle before. Hey, you know what else is pretty cool? I've never had a niece before either. And after next week I'm going to have two!"

She giggled but apparently couldn't keep the exciting news of an impending pony ride to herself. A second later she raced off to find her sister, leaving him alone with Allie.

"Thank you." His future sister-in-law gifted him with one of her sweet smiles and threaded her arm through his.

"For what?"

"Everything. Offering them a pony ride and allowing her to call you Uncle Wyatt. And especially for agreeing to host the wedding here. I know it's been a hassle."

Wyatt shrugged, uncomfortable with her gratitude. "No problem. Until you two finish that house you're building, my place is the biggest. It just make sense to have it here. Anyway, it's not every day a guy's older brother manages to marry a woman worlds better than he deserves."

She smiled at that and gave his arm a squeeze. "You know, I thought I would be nervous having a bestselling author for a brother-in-law, but you're one of the best things to come out of this whole deal. I'm so glad you and Gage have mended your differences."

He didn't quite know how to answer that. He and Gage really hadn't had any differences to mend. They hadn't been estranged in the true sense of the word, only running on different tracks, separated by tragedy and the memory of a girl they had both been unable to protect.

Before he could answer, Gage hobbled across the deck toward him. Despite having broken both legs earlier in the summer, Gage was getting around pretty well, Wyatt thought. He'd lost the crutches a few weeks back, and though he still limped—and likely would for a while—it was hard to believe he'd been in a wheelchair until just a few months earlier.

Gage raised an eyebrow at their linked arms. "I turn my back long enough to throw the steaks on the grill and you're putting the moves on my girl," he growled. "Can't I trust you for two seconds?"

Wyatt grinned and pulled Allie closer. "I decided she's too good for a lowly, overworked Feeb like you. We're running away to Acapulco."

"Ah. Lovely," Allie said. "Just let me go pack my suntan lotion."

Gage leaned a hip against the railing. "What can he offer, besides this fancy ranch and all those ill-gotten millions he's earned with his little writing hobby?"

"There is that," Allie said with a grin.

Gage straightened and tugged her toward him. "I'm not a

famous writer, Al. Just a man who's crazy in love with you and your girls."

Gage might not be a writer but he definitely had a way with words, Wyatt thought, at least judging by sudden stars in his fiancée's eyes and the way she melted into his arms.

They shared a kiss, brief but tender enough to have Wyatt wondering if he ought to leave the two of them alone. Before he could, Anna—the younger of Allie's girls—ran over to them in tears.

"Mama, Gaby says she gets to ride the pony first. I want to ride first!"

Allie sent Wyatt an exasperated look before turning back to her daughter. "Neither of you will be riding any pony unless you learn to share."

She gave Gage one more quick kiss, then headed off to avert the crisis.

"She's wonderful, Gage," Wyatt said after she left. "And the girls are too. I'm really happy for you."

Gage sat in one of the Adirondack chairs on the deck and propped his left leg on the matching footstool. "I'm getting the better end of the deal and we both know it. I'm getting a gorgeous wife and two wonderful little girls. What's she getting, besides a cranky workaholic FBI agent?"

Wyatt sat beside him, his mind on the older brother he had worshiped and on all the years and distance between them.

"A good man," he murmured, then, uncomfortable with that line of conversation, he changed the subject. "Where's Dad?"

"He took over grill duties from me. Said it was so I could get off my feet, but Sam never could stand letting someone else char the meat when he's around."

Wyatt wasn't sure he'd ever known that about his father. For an instant, he resented that Gage knew their father so much better than he did, then he thought of Gage's relationship with Lynn and how strained it had been before this summer, when they had all begun to find peace.

They would never completely find it, he was afraid. There would always be a gaping hole in their world that would not be filled, but Wyatt wanted to think they had at last begun building a bridge across it.

"How long has it been since we've all been together like this?" he asked. "Mom, Dad, and you and I?"

Gage looked startled at the observation. "Too long," he said, his voice gruff, then apparently felt the need to change the subject himself. "How's the new book coming?"

The question inevitably brought his mind right back to Taylor, who hadn't been far from it in the two days since their kiss.

"It's taken a bit of a turn. Hunter Bradshaw's sister staunchly maintains her brother's innocence and she's asked me to help her prove it."

Gage raised an eyebrow at that piece of information, and Wyatt didn't miss the sudden speculation in his eyes.

"You plan to?"

He blew out a breath. "I don't know. I doubt we'll find out much, but I told Taylor I would do what I can. What do you know about the Ferrin murders?"

"Only what I read in the papers. As far as I know, the FBI wasn't involved in the investigation. Anyway, it happened before I transferred to the Salt Lake field office. Wasn't there a Liberty connection?"

"Eden, anyway. Mickie lived there for a while and practiced law in Ogden. Dru was my age and went to school with me." He paused, not sure why he felt compelled to tell his brother this. After a moment, he decided to go with his instincts. "Things weren't easy after Mom and I moved back here. I missed you and dad and I didn't have a lot of friends for a while. Dru was always a good one."

A muscle worked in Gage's jaw and Wyatt wondered what was going on inside his brother's mind.

"If you want," Gage said after a minute, "I can talk to the investigating officer at the police department, see if there were any dead-end leads that maybe should have been looked at a little more closely."

Though warmed by the offer, Wyatt still shook his head. "Thanks but I can't ask you to do that. You've got enough on your plate right now. In less than a week you're going to be not only a brand-new husband but an instant father."

Gage caught sight of his wife chasing across the lawn after one of the girls and grinned. "I'm a lucky bastard, aren't I?"

Wyatt grinned back, thrilled to see his brother so happy. This Gage seemed completely different from the grim, taciturn man he used to be. Right then, Wyatt wanted to chase after Allie and give her a great big smack on the lips for all she'd done for his brother.

"Yeah, you are. Anyway, you don't need another case to investigate on the side."

Gage's grin slid away at the unspoken reminder of the one case Wyatt knew he would never stop working.

"It won't hurt me to ask a few questions," Gage replied. "I could use something to keep me busy this week before the wedding. Maybe I can turn up a new angle for you. Wouldn't want you to disappoint this Taylor woman."

As much as he didn't want to disappoint her either, Wyatt was very much afraid that's exactly what would happen.

Chapter 6

Taylor decided within two minutes of meeting Stacy Hernandez she didn't like the other woman.

She wasn't sure exactly what set her teeth on edge—maybe the news reporter's perky, blindingly white smile or the way she constantly tilted that smile in Wyatt's direction like a dying flower on a windowsill turning toward the sun.

Or maybe it was just the avid speculation in her big brown eyes as she took in the two of them together.

The moment they met her at Red Rocks, a downtown brew pub, Taylor's instant impression was of someone ambitious and cagey. A lot like the Dru Ferrin she remembered.

"I'm surprised to see the two of you together," the reporter said after she had placed her order for low-carb pizza and a diet soda. Wyatt ordered one of the pub's famous beers and Taylor settled for a bottled water.

"You make an odd dynamic duo, if you don't mind me saying," she went on. "The sister of Utah's most infamous murderer and the state's author *du jour.* How did this come about?"

"It's a long story," Wyatt answered, to Taylor's relief, as she was just about to tell the reporter to mind her own business.

Stacy angled her not inconsiderable cleavage in his direction. "I suppose you're writing a book about the murders. I'm sure it's going to be great. They were *so* horrific. The shooting of a pregnant TV personality and her dying mother makes pretty sensational copy, I have to admit."

"Sensational copy isn't everything," he answered coldly.

For a woman who made her living communicating with people, the reporter seemed completely oblivious to the bite in his voice. She didn't so much as blink.

"I'm not sure how I feel about you tagging along today," she went on—and though her words directed at Wyatt might have sounded unwelcoming, the warm smile and meaningful look she sent him under her impossibly long eyelashes told a vastly different story.

"Oh?"

"I agreed to talk to Hunter Bradshaw's sister." She turned to Taylor. "To be frank, I was hoping we could work something out. You scratch my back and all that. I share what I remember about Dru and her state of mind before her death and in return, you help me score a jailhouse interview with your brother."

"Hunter's not giving any interviews right now to anyone except Wyatt," Taylor said.

The reporter sipped at the diet soda the waiter delivered to their table. "I'm not sure I want to show up in a book about the case."

"You won't." Wyatt's voice was firm. "We're just looking for background. Perhaps an angle the police might have overlooked."

"If I can't have access to Hunter, what can you offer me if I agree to talk to you?"

"What do you want?" Wyatt countered.

Taylor had an inkling what the reporter was after by the sudden light in her eyes as she took in his lean good looks. This time Wyatt seemed the oblivious one.

"An exclusive," Stacy said after a moment. "I want to know the minute Hunt Bradshaw files an appeal. I also want to know if you nail down anything about what Dru was working on before her death. I want to be on the inside track with his appellate team."

Wyatt inclined his head to Taylor, subtly pointing out that she was the one in control, at least when it came to her brother's case and monitoring who had access to it.

Taylor might have wished she could tell Stacy Hernandez just what she could do with that perky smile and those flirtatious looks but she knew if she wanted to find any answers she had to play her game.

The woman might have valuable information about the case. If they wanted access to that information, they would have to offer something in return.

"We can arrange that," Taylor said.

"Okay. What do you want to know?"

Taylor glanced at the legal pad where she had prepared a list of questions. "I've heard from a few different people that you and Dru were good friends. Is that right?"

Stacy appeared to be thinking how best to answer that as she sipped at her soft drink. "Hard to say," she finally said. "Good friends? I don't know. I'm not sure Dru really had many good friends. She wasn't the kind of woman you called up at the last minute for a trip to the movies when you don't have a date, but yeah, I guess I was as close as she had to a friend at the station anyway."

"Did you have any idea she was seeing anyone besides my brother?"

Stacy shrugged. "I knew. I got the impression he was unavailable, if you know what I mean."

"Married?" Wyatt asked.

"Yeah. She didn't say that in so many words but I definitely picked up the adultery vibe there."

"Did she ever mention a name?" Taylor pressed. "Did you ever meet him?"

"No and no. Wish I could help you there but Dru was pretty closemouthed about the whole thing. Maybe that's why I thought the man was married. She had no problem telling me all about your brother—Hunter the hottie—but not much at all about this mystery man."

Her expression turned pensive. "Although as I told the police during the investigation, there was this one day when I heard her on the phone with somebody. This sounds like it's right out of a soap opera, but I swear she said something like *'If you don't tell your wife, I will.'* Maybe it wasn't quite that dramatic but that was the gist of it."

What if Dru had threatened her married lover with exposure—and if said married lover wasn't exactly thrilled about it? Wouldn't that make a good motive for murder? Taylor wondered.

"Can you think of anyone else she might have confided in about the man's identity?" Wyatt asked.

"Not really. At least not at the station. Like I said, I was the closest thing she had to a friend there."

She paused while the waiter delivered their order, then

took a bite of pizza before continuing. "You know, I got the distinct impression the guy was a cop, too. Makes sense since she met a lot of cops on the crime beat. That's how she met your brother, right?"

Taylor nodded tightly. She couldn't help thinking that if Dru Ferrin had been assigned to a different beat—one far removed from the police department—the orbit of her world never would have collided with Hunter's and her brother wouldn't currently be sitting on death row.

"What about any stories Dru might have been working on before her death?" she asked.

"I don't know, but if you find anything out, I want it. Whatever she had in the pipeline, Dru seemed to think it would be huge. She dropped a few hints that this one would be her ticket to network news, but that was it."

"And you have no idea what it might have been about?"

"Believe me, after she died, I tried everything I could think of to find out. I scoured her computer looking for her notes, I read through every notebook I could find. But she must have kept anything she had in some secret location. Whatever it was, the story died along with her since she apparently hadn't taken anybody else into her confidence. Even the news director didn't have a clue."

"If you had to make a guess, what direction would you think?" Wyatt asked. "Drugs? Organized crime?"

The reporter chewed and swallowed a tiny bite of pizza. "I'm just giving impressions here, nothing solid and nothing you could ever quote me on, but a few weeks before her death she suddenly seemed fascinated with the police procedures code. She studied it all the time. I remember wondering at the time if she might have been working some kind of in-depth story about the police department."

Taylor thought of the police corruption incident Hunter had been involved with and the enemies he had made because of reporting it. What if Dru's story was linked to it somehow, and if the corruption went deeper than just that isolated case? If Dru were about to go public with a story about police corruption, any number of people could have a motive to want her dead—and the means to arrange things behind the scene so that someone else took the blame for it.

"What about death threats?" Taylor asked. "My brother says he gave Dru his personal weapon because she had received some kind of warning."

Stacy shrugged. "Could be. She received death threats on a regular basis. Dru's approval ratings with viewers might have been through the roof but the sources she reported on weren't all that crazy about her."

"Did you see or hear any threats made against her?" Wyatt asked.

"Nothing stands out. Not that I can remember anyway. Look, it's a hazard of the job, especially for an aggressive, in-your-face reporter like Dru. I've got a whole drawer full of my own lovely collection of angry letters. Most of the time you just have to shrug off the crazies. But if she was worried enough about it to talk her big bad cop boyfriend about protection, maybe this time she thought somebody was serious."

"You never saw her with the gun in her possession though?" Taylor pressed.

Stacy laughed. "Sorry I can't make it that easy for you. Don't you think I would have come forward during the original investigation or the trial if I'd had that kind of information to share? I'm not saying I believe your brother was telling the truth about giving Dru his gun, just that it wasn't completely improbable."

She took one more bite of pizza—leaving most of it on her plate—swallowed another sip of cola and stood up. "As fun as this has been, I'm going to have to run. I'm doing a live feed on the six o'clock broadcast. Sorry to cut things short. Thanks for the pizza—and remember, I'm going to want an exclusive on this. Call me if you think you have anything I could use."

This last was directed at Wyatt—and Taylor had a pretty good idea Stacy was talking about sharing more than just information.

She pushed away her unreasonable jealousy as the reporter walked out of the pub. She had no right to feel territorial about Wyatt. They had shared one kiss, that was all. Okay, so her toes still hadn't uncurled three days later but she preferred to focus on the woman's revelations, not on her own unwilling attraction to Wyatt.

Of course, it was a little hard to ignore that attraction when the two of them were sitting together on one side of the table. She thought of moving to the other side but she knew that would look foolish and only bring more attention to the sudden physical tension she, at least, sensed simmering between them.

"Do you see what I mean?" she said to Wyatt, trying hard to ignore the heat radiating from him. "The police should have followed up on these leads. Any number of people had far more motive to kill Dru Ferrin than Hunter did—the father of her baby, for one, if she really threatened to go to his wife about their affair. Whoever she was about to implicate in her big story, for another. Whoever made those death threats. The list is endless."

"We don't know much more now than we did an hour ago," he pointed out.

Taylor bristled. "We know Dru's lover was married. We know she might have been doing a story about police corruption. We know she had received death threats in the past so it was perfectly plausible that she could have asked Hunter for a weapon."

"Speculation. I'm afraid that's all we've got. Still, I would like to know how seriously the police considered these other possibilities before focusing on Hunter."

"So would I." She was quiet for a moment. "So where do we go from here?"

"Good question. I told you my brother is an FBI agent. I told him about the case and he offered to take a look at the case file, see if anything unusual leaps out. Maybe he can dig around and see if there were any murmurs of a big police corruption story around the time of the murders."

At his offer, any lingering annoyance vanished and it took all her willpower to keep from flinging her arms around his neck. "That would be wonderful!" she exclaimed.

"I don't know that he'll find anything," Wyatt warned.

"I can't tell you how much your help means to me."

His gaze met hers and something in those grey-green depths reminded her forcibly of the kiss they had shared. For just an instant, she was back in her office, pressed tightly against her desk, her body wrapped around him.

She inhaled a sharp breath, willing the image away.

"I'd better go." Her voice sounded low, husky, so she cleared her throat and tried again. "I've got class tonight."

She thought he might have looked disappointed that she was rushing off, but he quickly veiled whatever emotion flickered in those eyes.

"I'll be in touch to let you know if Gage comes up with any leads."

"Great. And I'll keep you updated on my end of things. Thank you again."

With one last hesitant smile, she hurried from the pub before she did something absolutely stupid like kiss that mouth she'd been dreaming about for days.

"I wish you could come with me."

Taylor forced a smile for Kate, though she was afraid her skin might crack with the effort. "I would love to. You know I would—you're going to have a wonderful experience. But I don't think the other doctors in Operation Care would be all that crazy about having a med school dropout hanging around taking up space at their Guatemala clinics."

Kate folded her favorite pair of jeans and tucked them into her already-bulging suitcase. "They would be lucky to have you." Her voice rang with conviction. "You're a better doctor even without a degree than most of the residents at the hospital."

Taylor smiled at her roommate, touched by her loyalty, however misguided. She meant what she said—she would love to be going along with Kate. In just over an hour, she was leaving for a two-week trip with a group of doctors and nurses to provide medical care to poverty-stricken villages in central America.

This was Kate's second trip to Guatemala—the second of what Taylor knew would be many. Her last trip six months ago had been one of those life-changing moments for Kate. Taylor knew she loved the chance to help others, to relieve suffering among some of the most poor and humble people on earth. When she came back, Kate had glowed for weeks.

That ugly envy Taylor hated so much crawled around inside her skin. While Kate was bringing hope and healing, Taylor was stuck here with her law books and her endless briefs and this hopeless, quixotic quest to save her brother's life.

She wanted so much to experience the pure joy of helping others, with no expectation of reward other than a grateful smile. With great effort, she did her best to hide her envy. She would hate it if Kate had even the tiniest suspicion how very much she wanted to stow away in that suitcase.

"Be careful," Taylor said with a teasing smile. "Don't let any sexy Latin Romeo steal your heart so you won't want to come back."

"Oh, like that will happen." She paused, and the laughter in her eyes faded, replaced by sudden concern. "Anyway, I think your heart's in far more danger than mine right now."

To her chagrin, Taylor felt heat creep across her skin. "Mine? Don't worry, my heart is perfectly safe."

"Is it?" Kate asked, doubt in her voice.

"Of course. Why wouldn't it be?"

"Oh no reason. When is your next meeting with our favorite sexy author?"

She could feel the heat of her blush turn into an inferno and knew by the sudden knowing look Kate gave her that she must be bright red.

"Tomorrow. He called a few hours ago to arrange a meeting. His brother Gage works for the FBI. He knows a sergeant at the police department who wants to talk to us. Apparently this cop wasn't happy with the investigation and never believed Hunter was guilty. When he found out Wyatt was writing a book about the case he talked to Gage, who arranged for us to talk to him about what he knows."

Her explanation wound down. "What is it? What's the matter" she asked when she saw Kate stopped packing and was standing in the middle of the floor, a belt in her hands.

"What did you say was the name of Wyatt's brother?"

"Gage. Gage McKinnon. Do you know him?"

"I don't know. That name sure seems familiar. I wonder if I've met him through the hospital somehow."

"Maybe you could have bumped into him during an abuse investigation or something."

"Maybe." She shook her head a little as if to clear it. "Don't you hate that, when you hear a name of someone you're sure you've met but you have no idea where or when? It drives me crazy. Anyway, as worried as I am about you, I'm so thrilled to see you making progress on Hunter's case."

"It seems like a lot of things are happening after so many months of feeling like I was the lone voice in the wilderness proclaiming his innocence. I still don't know if it's enough, though. Martin still doesn't believe we have sufficient evidence for appeal and definitely not enough to get a new trial at this point."

"You finally talked to him?"

"Yes. He returned my call yesterday after canceling our appointment again this week. I told him about Wyatt helping me and the progress we were making. 'It sounds promising,' he said. That was about it."

"I don't imagine he was too thrilled about that. Martin's a little territorial when it comes to you and Hunter."

Taylor knew Kate didn't like Martin—she thought him arrogant and self-absorbed, but even she had to admit he was a good attorney. "He was one of our father's closest friends. He's protective, that's all."

Kate looked unconvinced but she didn't press the matter. She snapped shut the lid of her suitcase then hefted it to the floor. "I guess that's everything."

"I hope so because I don't think you could fit so much as one more a tube of lip balm in that thing."

Kate laughed. She opened her mouth to answer but was interrupted when Belle gave one sharp bark just seconds before Taylor heard the rustle of mail in the old-fashioned slot in the front door. She should have known. Belle rarely barked—only quick greetings for the newspaper carrier and for the long-suffering mail carrier.

"Will you check that?" Kate asked. "I was hoping my paycheck would be here before I left so I could deposit it on the way to the airport."

"Of course."

Being envious of Kate for this opportunity was a normal emotion, she told herself as she walked through the house toward the mail slot in the front door. If she wasn't envious, then she could worry. That would mean she had completely given up her dream of being a doctor.

The only way law school was bearable was if she reminded herself it was only temporary, that someday, when Hunter was vindicated and was out of prison, she would be free to take her hopes and dreams from the shelf, polish them up and try again.

In the meantime, she would do her best to hide how very much she longed to be in Kate's size-seven shoes right now.

She scooped up the mail from the floor and quickly leafed through the bills and junk mail. "Your paycheck's here," she called out.

"That's a relief," Kate replied from the other room. "My poor Visa can't take much more abuse right now. Anything else good?"

Taylor stopped at an odd piece of mail, a small manila envelope with no return address and her name typed on the cover. Curious about it, she left the other mail on the hall table and used a fingernail to open the seal.

She wasn't sure why but sudden foreboding flickered through her. She shrugged it off and pulled out the contents.

For one shocked second, she could only stare as her heartbeat seemed to slow then burst into hyperspeed. Confusion and revulsion and thick, jabbing fear fought within her.

She knew this picture, had seen it as evidence during the trial, though she had hoped never to have to see it again. The image was seared into her memory—two women, one sickly, frail to the point of emaciation, lying in bed, the other, pregnant and blond, sprawled across her as if trying to protect her. There was blood everywhere—on the bed, on the wall, great pools of it on the floor.

The crime-scene photos of Dru Ferrin and her mother was stark, horrible. A nightmare she had tried hard to forget.

What was one doing in her mailbox?

She drew in a deep breath trying to force oxygen back into her lungs. There was a message for her, she realized, typed in heavy black letters on a piece of plain paper.

YOUR BROTHER IS A MURDERER. LET HIS VICTIMS REST IN PEACE, UNLESS YOU WANT TO END UP LIKE THEM.

She was still trying to force her mind to wade through the horror when Kate walked into the living room, suitcase in tow.

"I guess I'll see you in ten days, then." Her roommate grinned. "I would tell you to take advantage of having the house to yourself by engaging in a little recreational activity with the sexy and charming Wyatt McKinnon, except I know you won't take my advice."

Taylor barely heard her. Who had sent the letter? Who wanted her to stop the investigation?

Fear slithered through her, black and slick and ugly. She drew in another deep breath then realized Kate was waiting for some kind of response.

She tried to force her scattered thoughts to coalesce but she didn't act fast enough, apparently, judging by the sudden concern on Kate's features.

"What's wrong? You're looking about two shades away from hypoxic right now."

She couldn't tell her, Taylor realized. Kate would cancel her entire trip to stay home with her if she had any idea about the threat.

Maybe she and Wyatt had touched a nerve somehow—maybe they were closer to the truth than either of them realized.

"It's nothing. I'm fine." She forced a smile, hoping she was a good enough actress to fool Kate for five more minutes. "You need to eat something. Would you like me to heat you some soup?"

As a diversionary tactic, her question couldn't have worked better. "I don't have time." Kate glanced at her watch. "Jeez, I'm supposed to be at the airport in twenty minutes. I'll pick something up when I get there."

"Make sure you do. Who knows when you'll have a chance to eat again. Airlines don't even serve peanuts anymore."

"Yes, Mother." Kate grinned at her then rushed for the door, dragging her heavy suitcase behind her.

"Be safe," Taylor murmured to her friend.

"Right back at you, honey."

Kate shoved the suitcase into the trunk of her Honda then climbed in and drove away. Taylor stood in the doorway watching her go, the grisly envelope in her hand and cold fear in her stomach.

Chapter 7

"Okay, spill. What's going on?"

Wyatt held the question in check as long as he could but it finally erupted ten minutes after he pick up an edgy, ill-at-ease Taylor.

She shifted from her perusal of the leaves drifting down in front of his Tahoe to look at him. In her blue eyes he saw wariness and those dark, uneasy shadows.

"Nothing's out of the ordinary. Why do you ask?"

"I don't know. Maybe because you're about as jittery as spring calves on branding day."

"I'm fine. Just a little preoccupied, that's all."

"Is that why you haven't said three words to me since I picked you up?" he asked.

"I believe I just said several more than three," she said primly.

Wyatt grimaced. "Thank you for pointing that out, Counselor."

She almost smiled but it slid away before she would give it a chance to form.

"I'm sorry. It's been a...crazy few days. I've got a million things running through my mind today. It's almost midterms and I have so much work to do."

"Oh. And here I thought maybe you were nervous because you couldn't stop thinking about the kiss."

She blinked, obviously astonished that he would finally bring up the subject they had both been skirting around for nearly a week.

"I've completely forgotten about that," she responded quickly—so quickly that his admittedly fragile male ego might even have believed her and been shattered...except for the rosy blush that spread from her neck to the roots of her auburn hair.

He swallowed a smile instead. "Have you now?"

She refused to meet his gaze. "Believe it or not," she snapped, "I do have other things to do besides sit around thinking about...about kissing you. I do have a life."

He had a life too, and plenty of other things that should be occupying his mind—his book deadline, the publicity tour his agent was pushing for, his ranch and his tangled family relationships.

He knew he should be busy thinking about all kinds of other topics but he couldn't seem to work his mind around much else but that kiss they had shared.

He wasn't sure how he had contained himself from trying for another taste during their interview with the reporter earlier in the week. He might have tried when they were alone after the interview if Taylor hadn't run away so quickly.

"I've been thinking about it," he surprised himself by admitting. "I've been thinking about it a lot."

"Well, cut it out," she mumbled.

He laughed at her command. "I'll do my best," he lied. In truth, though he recognized the danger of it, he *liked* thinking about it, remembering her sweetly uninhibited response. Wondering when he might have the chance to taste that sultry mouth again.

"If you're not thinking about the kiss, what's troubling you? And don't lie and say everything's fine."

Her gaze shifted from him to the changing landscape out the window, then back to him. He had the strong feeling she wanted to confide in him but he could almost watch her change her mind.

"I'm struggling with a couple of my classes," she answered, with what he was sure was a lie. "That's all. My toughest class in med school was a piece of cake compared to some of this coursework."

"Because your heart isn't in law school the same way it was set on becoming a doctor."

"That's not true!"

"No?"

She sighed. "Well, maybe it's a little true. My heart might not want to be in law school but my head knows I don't have any choice. I've learned through hard experience that it's better to pay attention to my head."

Was that a warning for him? Wyatt wondered.

He didn't need it. Not really. He might tease her about that heated kiss they had shared but he knew damn well repeating it would be disastrous all the way around.

"Smart policy," he murmured. "Sounds like maybe you do have a little lawyer in you after all."

She sent him a swift, unreadable look but said nothing, and a moment later he reached their destination.

He pulled into the driveway of the modest house in one of the nicer neighborhoods in Sugarhouse, behind a couple of bikes and a big four-wheel-drive pickup.

Mike Thurman met them at the door. The cop was stocky but solid, in his early forties with wavy dark hair and dark sideburns. He had a veteran cop's confident, bring-it-on stance.

"You McKinnon's brother?" he asked.

He and Gage had spent so much of their lives on entirely different tracks, it seemed odd to be lumped together into such a neat package.

"Yes," he answered. "I'm Wyatt McKinnon and this is Taylor Bradshaw."

"Detective Bradshaw's sister. I know. I saw you at the trial. I'm sorry things went down the way they did, ma'am."

"Thank you. I am too."

"I never believed he did it. Your brother is a good man and a good cop. The kind I'd want watching my back."

Tears bloomed in her eyes before she blinked them away and gave the man a radiant smile. "Thank you."

"Same goes for yours." Thurman turned back to Wyatt. "I was part of the task force earlier in the summer that was trying to arrest that A-hole Juber when he gunned his truck and went after your brother. If I'd have been another foot or two to the left, I would have been crushed right alongside your brother."

"Your brother was crushed?" Taylor asked, her eyes wide with concern. "Is he all right?"

"He was in rough shape for a while," Wyatt answered. "The accident broke both of his legs, but he was lucky none of his internal organs were damaged."

"He's getting around better now," Thurman said. "When

he dropped by the other day, I was surprised to see him moving around on crutches. A hit like that, I figured he'd be in a wheelchair for the better part of a year."

"Gage can be a stubborn cuss," Wyatt answered. "He lost the chair as soon as possible. Before he probably should have."

Thurman seemed to remember his manners. "Sorry to leave you standing out here. Come in." He opened the door wide. "We've got the place to ourselves. The wife and the kids went to a movie. They should be gone for a couple hours at least."

He led them into a comfortable, lived-in looking family room. School backpacks cluttered a table near the door and toys were jumbled in one corner, as if somebody had done a quick pickup job.

It all seemed so *normal*, like his family's house always looked when he was growing up, before Charley's kidnapping. Their house in Liberty had been small and cramped, filled to the brim with Gage's remote-control cars, Wyatt's books, Charley's stuffed animals.

When they moved to Las Vegas so Sam McKinnon could open his own cabinetry shop, their house had seemed huge and comfortable, with an entire playroom for their stuff. That summer, he remembered, the room had always been cluttered. There was always a card table set up with some project or other on it—an erector set creation, a jigsaw puzzle, a model airplane waiting for glue.

Like everything else, Charlotte's kidnapping had changed that too. After she was taken, the playroom stayed immaculate, virtually unused for that year before Lynn and Sam had separated.

Neither he nor Gage ever seemed to want to spend much time in there. He remembered they had tried a few times but it had been too empty without a curly-haired girl coloring on the floor in front of the TV or begging for attention.

."Thank you for seeing us," Taylor said into the sudden awkward silence, and Wyatt realized he had let his mind slide too easily along familiar grim channels.

"Gage said you had some information about the Ferrin murders," he said as an opener.

The cop suddenly looked wary. "Maybe. But if I talk to you, this all has to be off-the-record. I'm three years away from my pension. I can't be too careful."

"Of course," Wyatt said, intrigued by the man's words and by his sudden nervousness. "Whatever you tell us stays here. If I need anything for the book, I'll find a corroborating source."

Thurman still looked reluctant to talk and Wyatt wondered if this trip had been in vain.

"Please." Taylor sat forward, her eyes pleading, though her voice was quiet. "If you know something that might help clear my brother, please tell us."

After a moment, Thurman nodded slowly. "I have to trust you'll do right by me," he said, looking at Wyatt. "Your brother is a stand-up guy, so I have to hope you're the same."

Wyatt decided he liked being lumped together with Gage, at least in this instance.

"I knew Dru Ferrin pretty well," Thurman announced.

Wyatt and Taylor exchanged glances and he could see the same question forming in her blue eyes. Was this the married man she'd been having an affair with?

Something of their suspicion must have shown, because Thurman rose to his feet quickly. "Not like that! If either of you knew my wife, the thought that I would ever dare cheat on her would never enter your mind. No, this was different."

He paused, then sat down again. "I was working with Dru on a story. I was a confidential informant, I guess you could say, kind of like what we're doing now."

Wyatt sat forward. "What kind of story was she working on?"

"A huge one. She said she thought it would be the biggest of her career. Her big break. I think it might have been the reason someone killed her, because she knew too much."

"About what?" Taylor sat forward eagerly in anticipation.

"Corruption in the police department. Corruption so deep it makes the Grand Canyon look like an irrigation ditch."

"What kind of corruption?" Wyatt asked.

"You name it. Payoffs, extortion. Evidence that goes unreported or even evidence that gets manufactured. I'm not saying it's endemic or widespread, only that a few select people in positions of power have created their own little kingdoms."

"Dru was working on a story about this?" Wyatt asked.

"She wanted to blow the lid off," the cop answered. "I think she saw it as a personal crusade."

Taylor thought of the case Hunter had been involved in. It had happened during the time he dated Dru—maybe she had learned about it and decided to investigate further.

"You were her source?" she asked.

"Not the only one but probably the main one."

"Why did you talk to Dru?"

"I've been with this department half my life," Thurman answered. "I love the men and women I work with, love the badge. And I hate seeing a few of my so-called superiors crap all over that badge."

Hunter had been just as angry about the corruption he had witnessed, she remembered. He had loved being a cop; like Thurman he'd loved the badge. He considered being a cop both an honor and a privilege.

"I talked to Dru at least a half-dozen times in the few months before her death. Last I talked to her, she said she was putting the finishing touches on her story."

"Do you think someone killed her to shut her up?" Taylor asked, excitement growing within her. This was it, she thought. This was the smoking gun, the missing link.

"I can believe that theory a hell of a lot more easily than I believe Hunter Bradshaw could kill two women in cold blood. Besides, did you see anybody else do a story on police corruption after her death? No. The whole thing died along with her."

"Why didn't you tell someone else?" Wyatt asked.

"Would *you?* I told Dru and she ended up dead, along with her mother. I haven't dared tell anyone else. For all I know, just telling you could put your lives in danger."

Taylor thought of the threatening note sent to her and ice crept along her nerve endings.

"Seems to me, if you had these kind of suspicions, you should have gone to Internal Affairs. Especially after two women were killed."

The skepticism in Wyatt's voice drew Taylor's gaze and she realized he didn't appear nearly as convinced as she was that the news of police corruption was significant.

"I don't know how deep it goes. For all I knew, I would be next for going public. Look what happened to Hunter—and all he did was step forward about one isolated incident. I got a wife and kids to think about."

"Why do you think Dru was killed over this particular story?" Wyatt asked.

"I don't. But a day or so before she died, she called me, scared about a death threat she received. Said whoever called sounded serious. She didn't know if it was related to the corruption story but she didn't know what else it would have been about. She warned me to watch my back." Regret darkened his eyes. "I only wish I'd been able to do more to watch hers."

"You suspected someone involved in the corruption story

to be responsible for her death. And yet you let Hunter Bradshaw go to death row for it."

"It's been eating me up inside since his conviction. But look at it from my perspective. I had no proof of anything, just suspicions. Who could I tell? The detectives on the case reported directly to their superiors—the same superiors who had their hand in a lot of very illegal pies."

"What about outside the department? The FBI or the department of public safety."

"I lost my nerve after Dru's death and decided to just wait out my last few years before retirement."

"So why talk to us now?"

"I can't live with myself anymore. Every day I wonder if an innocent man is on death row. When Gage brought up the case with me and said you were writing a book, I knew I had to find the stones to step forward."

"Do you believe him?" Taylor asked after they finished their interview and were once more in Wyatt's Tahoe heading toward her house.

Wyatt was quiet for several moments as they drove down the wide city streets. "I believe him," he said finally. "He has no real reason to tell us, and if he's right about how deep it goes, he has every reason to keep quiet, except to get the truth out."

"I hear a disclaimer in there," she said quietly.

"I don't believe anything he said could be a basis for appeal unless you had proof that whoever threatened Dru was connected to the police corruption—and that whoever it was followed up his threats with murder."

She had reached the same conclusion. "So we're back where we started."

At her glum tone, Wyatt reached across the seat until his fingers found hers. She knew it was likely foolish but she found enormous comfort in his touch.

"We're just getting started. Every piece of information we find is another piece of the puzzle. We just have to figure out where it fits—or if it belongs to a completely different picture."

She sighed, grateful for his perspective even as she found the truth of his words frustrating. She wasn't about to complain, though. In just a week of working with Wyatt, she knew more now than she had discovered alone in eighteen months.

Clearing her brother's name no longer seemed like some unreachable goal. Difficult, maybe. But difficult was much better than impossible.

"Thurman's right, though," Wyatt said, his tone suddenly grave. "If someone killed Dru to keep her from reporting about police corruption, they likely won't stop with her. We could be in danger."

Her hand tightened in his. How could she have forgotten that note, that terrible crime scene picture, even for a moment?

Someone in the police department would have access to official crime scene photos, she thought. They could easily lift it from the file and figure out a way to send it to her. Was it a coincidence that she received it in the mail right after Gage McKinnon arranged for them to talk to Mike Thurman?

"What's wrong?" Wyatt asked, seeming to notice her sudden tension.

She pulled her hand free as she debated telling him. How would he react? What if it made him leery of proceeding with the investigation?

No, she had to tell him. She had dragged him into this—it was unfair to withhold such significant information.

"Can you pull over?" she asked.

In the blue glow from the dashboard, she could see the odd look he sent her.

"Are you okay? You're not going to be sick, are you?" ·

"No." She clenched the strap of the leather bag that held her laptop, her notes from the interview and that terrible letter. "I need to show you something and I can't do it while we're driving."

"Yeah. Just let me find a good spot." A moment later he pulled into the parking lot of a convenience store. As he set the brake, she pulled the envelope from her bag.

"You asked me earlier why I was distracted. I did have a reason. A pretty good one. I've been worrying about this—"

She handed it to him, then waited nervously as he slid the picture out of the envelope. In the garish light from the convenience store, she saw a variety of emotions flit across his features—confusion, then surprise, then a raw, dangerous fury.

That look should have made her more nervous. There was no reason on earth she should have found solace in it, but she did.

"What is this?"

"I received it two days ago in the mail. No return address, obviously."

"Why didn't you tell me about it earlier?"

She should have, she saw that now. She had debated telling him for two days, even during their drive to Mike Thurman's house. She had a million excuses for not telling him, but she supposed the thing she had worried about most was that knowing about the threats would make him want to back out of helping her.

She realized now that that worry was unfounded. He might be concerned for her safety, but not his own.

"Did you go to the police?" he asked.

She shook her head. "No. I thought about calling Hunter's

partner, John Randall. He's still in the department and I've always thought of him as a decent, stand-up guy. I thought he could at least give me some direction for how to handle it, but in the end I decided against it. After talking to Sergeant Thurman, I have to think my instincts were right. I don't know if I can trust anyone in the police department now. Even John."

"I'll show it to Gage. He'll tell us what we should do from here. Any trace evidence on it has probably been compromised by now from you carrying it around for two days, but he might be able to find something."

Their fingers brushed as he handed it back to her and Taylor had to fight the urge to curl her hand around his and hang on tight.

"Let's get to your place and I'll call Gage and see if he can meet with us. He'll know what to do."

"Thank you," she said, when he had pulled out of the parking lot and headed in the direction of her house. "I'm afraid you didn't know what you were getting into when I dragged you into this."

"Maybe not. But it's going to make one hell of a story."

Right. The book about the case. How could she have forgotten? That was the only reason he was helping her, the sole reason for his concern. She needed to remember that and not fall into the seductive trap of thinking he might care about her.

The smell of smoke seared her nose when she opened the passenger door of Wyatt's vehicle after he pulled up in front of her house. A cold front had blown out of the Wasatch Mountains the night before—the Saunders must have started a fire in their woodstove. It would be just the thing to take the edge off a nippy fall evening.

The smell intensified as she climbed out of the truck. She frowned. Something was wrong. This was too strong, too acrid, to be woodsmoke from a fireplace.

She heard Belle give a low, frantic-sounding bark from around the back of the house—and then realization hit her.

The smoke wasn't coming from any of her neighbors' chimneys. It was billowing out of her bedroom window!

Chapter 8

Wyatt was already reaching for his cell phone and punching in 911. "Anybody inside?" he asked Taylor.

Her face had lost all color and she stared at him for a moment like she'd forgotten who he was.

"Taylor?" he prompted urgently.

She blinked a little and seemed to snap back. "No. No one's inside. My roommate is in Guatemala for another week."

A dog's frantic barking ripped through the night, and he saw her eyes go wide with horror.

"Belle! She still in there! I've got to get her!"

She pushed past him toward the front door, and Wyatt nearly had to tackle her to keep her from rushing into the flames he could now see licking through the front of the house.

"No! You can't go inside."

"I have to get her. Hunter loves her. I can't let her die. I can't!" She fought against his restraining arm, but he held tight.

"Look, you talk to Dispatch. I'll try to get the dog out. Where do you keep her when you're not home? What part of the house?"

"The kitchen. Right inside the back door."

He handed her his cell phone, where the dispatcher's voice still buzzed, trying to get information. "Stay here. Promise me, Tay. Stay here and wait for the fire department."

She nodded tightly as the dog's barking grew more frantic. "Please hurry!"

Someone else must have reported the fire, he thought as he headed around the back of the house. Sirens wailed in the distance. Common sense told him he should wait for the professionals to come and save the dog, but he didn't know how long it would take them to reach the scene—or how fast that fire was moving.

The flames hadn't made it to this part of the house yet, he saw with relief when he reached the back door, though smoke seeped out from around the door frame.

The dog's barking was louder now, frantic and wild, and she was scratching against the door so hard it shook.

Wyatt tugged the door handle but it wouldn't budge. Damn. He should have thought to have Taylor give him the key, but then, given the urgency of the situation, now probably wasn't the greatest time to have to mess with a lock.

"Hang on, pup," he called to the dog, though he knew Belle likely couldn't hear him over her barking and the growl of the flames. With tension seething through his veins like that smoke, he scanned Taylor's small brick patio for anything he could use to break into the house. He finally settled on a heavy clay planter.

Taylor wouldn't mind the sacrifice for the greater good, he knew, so he lifted the planter and swung it with a mighty heave through the small window inset in the door.

The window shattered with a crash and smoke instantly billowed out in a thick gray cloud.

Wyatt dug his mouth and nose into his jacket, then reached inside to work the lock. His fingers fumbled with it for a moment but he finally heard a click and it slid free.

The instant he wrenched open the door, a furry russet shape bolted out and raced toward a corner of the backyard, her barks frenzied and determined now instead of frightened.

What was she barking at? he wondered. The dog had just escaped a fiery death and her first thought was to chase after a stray cat?

"Come on, Belle," he called. The dog snarled once more into the darkness, then hurried to follow him as Wyatt made his way around the crackling flames.

They arrived around the front of the house just as a ladder truck pulled up. Taylor gasped with relief when she saw Wyatt and Belle, and dropped to her knees in the grass to embrace the dog.

When she looked up again, her eyes were dark with emotion. "Oh, Wyatt. Thank you!"

He wasn't a hero. He wanted to tell her to stop looking at him like he was, but before he could, a gruff-voiced firefighter decked out in full Nomex ordered them out of the way so crews could do their job.

Wyatt led her and the dog to a neighbor's yard, where they joined a gathering crowd.

Wyatt could imagine few things more heartbreaking than standing in the cool October night with Taylor, holding her while they watched the firefighters' feeble efforts to save her home and belongings. After a half hour of standing by helplessly, Wyatt could see now that their efforts would be in vain.

The fire burned too fast, too hot. At this rate, he would be surprised if even a wall was left standing.

She grew more quiet, more fragile, as the minutes ticked past, until now she stood next to him like a slim, silent wraith.

"I bought this house after my father died."

They were the first words she had whispered in at least ten minutes and he could barely hear her over the cacophony of flames and firefighters. He said nothing, just tightened his arm around her, wishing he could do more.

"Hunter moved out years before, and our family home was too big after the Judge died for just me. I didn't want to rent some cold, impersonal apartment. This seemed like a good compromise—close to the hospital and downtown. I loved being part of a neighborhood. Mowing the lawn on Saturday mornings, taking muffins over when someone was sick, painting and decorating. It was my escape from the pressures of med school—"

Her voice broke slightly on the last word, and Wyatt pulled her closer, turning her away from the fire to nestle against him. She slid her arms around his waist and tucked her head under his chin.

"I'm sorry, Taylor," he murmured, hating the inadequacy of the words.

"All my things were inside. Everything."

"The firefighters might be able to save some of it. You might find it's not a total loss."

She tilted her head to meet his gaze, and he saw stark reality in her blue eyes. She said nothing but he could see she knew his words were mere platitudes, that the fire would leave very little once its destructive power burned out.

He hated that he couldn't fix this for her. He wanted so much to spare her this loss, to make all the devastation disappear. He pulled her tighter, stunned and unnerved by the tenderness settling in his chest.

What had happened to his much-vaunted objectivity? Somehow in the last week everything had changed. Right now, with her in his arms, he knew he had been kidding himself.

He couldn't be cool and distant with Taylor Bradshaw. He had known from those very first days of the trial that she brought out this impulse to protect, to hold her close and keep her safe.

That impulse sharpened at the approach of a man wearing a fire department uniform but without protective gear. The man was lean and tough with graying hair, piercing blue eyes and a nickel-sized scar on one cheek. From a flying cinder? Wyatt wondered.

"Are you the owners of the dwelling?" he asked in a voice roughened by the acrid smoke.

Taylor pulled out of Wyatt's arms, color staining her pale cheeks. "I'm Taylor Bradshaw. I live here."

"Chief inspector Kirby," the man said. "While the crews are finishing up here, can you tell me if you have any idea how the fire might have started?"

In the flickering glow from the fire and the flashing emergency lights, her eyes were wide, distressed. "I don't know. We smelled smoke when we returned from a meeting, so I assume it started while we were gone."

She gave a helpless shrug that made Wyatt want to pull her close again.

"I've been trying to think if I left anything on—an appliance or something—but I can't think what it might be. I wasn't cooking or ironing or anything else like that before we left. I'm sorry I can't be more help."

"We'll get to the bottom of it," Kirby said, and Wyatt wondered if he was only imagining the implied accusation in the statement.

"Ms. Bradshaw has been with me for the past two hours interviewing a source for a book. I can personally vouch for her whereabouts during that time and so can our source if necessary."

The fire inspector turned probing blue eyes in his direction. "And you are?"

"Wyatt McKinnon. I'm a friend."

The ice in those eyes thawed slightly and Wyatt was slightly embarrassed to see recognition of his name there.

"I've enjoyed your books," the inspector said. "Especially *Point of Origin*."

"Why would you need to vouch for my whereabouts?" Taylor asked suddenly, before Wyatt could respond. "Am I some kind of suspect or something?"

Her frown deepened, and Wyatt saw the same grim conclusion he had arrived at some time earlier dawn in her eyes. "You think the fire was set deliberately?"

The inspector seemed far more friendly now—compassionate, even—as he turned back to her. "It's too soon to say for certain, ma'am, but I can tell you there are signs that certainly point in that direction. By all indications, an accelerant was used near the southeast corner of the house. We found traces of gasoline spilled around the foundation where the fire is burning most intensely. We'll know better when it cools and we can do a trace analysis."

"That's impossible! Who would do this?"

"That's something we'll do our best to find out, ma'am."

Another fire official called his name and gestured for him. Kirby nodded tightly to them and hurried away with a long, ground-eating stride.

"This can't be happening." Despite her height, Taylor looked small and frightened standing in the cold, her eyes devastated. "Why would anyone want to do this to me?"

From the extensive research he did for a book he had written about a northern California town terrorized for month by an arsonist, Wyatt knew the deadliest fires happened in the middle of the night when people were generally sleeping. By the time the smoke woke them, sometimes it was too late to escape.

An early evening fire would probably cause mostly property damage—that's the time of day when people were usually awake, fixing dinner, watching television, just going about the business of life. They were alert to their environment and would most likely be able to smell smoke and escape in time.

His gut told him this fire wasn't meant to hurt her. He couldn't help thinking about the note she received. Maybe the fire was a more sinister variation on the same theme.

"A warning?" he asked quietly.

She stared at him for one long, stark second, then realization clicked into her eyes. If possible, she paled a few more shades, and would have sagged to the ground if he hadn't reached for her.

"Let's just slow down here," he said, kicking himself for his bluntness, for springing his suspicions on her without warning. "We don't know anything yet. It might be arson, Kirby said. But then, it might be something else like wiring or a faulty furnace. We won't know until inspectors have time for a full investigation."

She looked ill. "Someone wants to stop us. We're getting too close. That's what this is about. It has to be."

"We don't know that."

"I know it." She closed her eyes. "What if I hadn't taken my laptop with me tonight? I would have lost everything!"

He remembered her office, all those neatly organized files. Hunter Central. "How much do you estimate you lost?"

"You saw the information I had. I had one full file cabinet with newspaper clippings and court documents. I'm going to have to start over collecting everything. There is nothing irreplaceable but it's going to take time for me to duplicate what I had."

He had to admit, he was inclined to believe the fire was connected to that threat she had received. If the fire didn't scare her away from investigating her brother's case—and from what he knew of Taylor Bradshaw, he knew it wouldn't—it would at least set her back.

He couldn't help wonder how many other twists and turns this case would take before they were done.

What a surreal experience, standing in the cold night air and watching her life go up in smoke.

Taylor wasn't sure how long she and Wyatt and Belle watched the fire crews valiantly fight to save her house. Time seemed distorted—rushing by one moment, then slowing to an excruciating crawl the next.

They were losing, though. She could see it in the faces of the firefighters, in the way the adrenaline spike they rode in on seemed to give way, first to a grim determination and then to a weary resignation.

The fire was mostly out—only a few hot spots remained—but through the smoke she at last could begin to see the extent of the damage that had been wrought. Only a few timbers of two skeletal walls remained. Everything else was gone.

Was this bleak devastation similar to what Hunter had felt after his arrest? She felt as if her entire life—twenty-six years—had just been snatched away from her.

Her father's desk, all her lovely books, the few mementos she had of her mother. Everything was gone.

She couldn't begin to process the devastating loss. Or how Kate was going to feel when she learned her home and belongings were gone forever, too.

"Do you and Belle have a place to stay?"

Wyatt's voice broke through her grim inventory, and Taylor blew out a long, exhausted breath. What would she have done without Wyatt's calm, steady presence? Throughout the entire ordeal he had stayed by her side, wiping away the stray tears that mortified her, supporting her during her brief conversations with firefighters, keeping her together when she feared she would shatter.

She was a mess even with him at her side—without him she knew she would probably be curled up in fetal position on the grass, sobbing her eyes out.

Still, for a moment she couldn't think how to answer his question. She could barely focus on enduring the next moment—forget about trying to figure out where she would sleep.

"My family has a cabin in Little Cottonwood Canyon. A house, really. Hunter lived there, but it's been empty since his arrest."

"You can't stay up there by yourself."

She blinked at his firm tone. "Why not? I've been staying here by myself since Kate went to Guatemala."

"That was before someone torched your house."

"I can't stay in some impersonal hotel," she said. "What would I do with Belle?"

"Come home with me."

She stared at him, stunned by the offer.

"I don't want you to be alone, Taylor. You shouldn't have to be. I have more than enough room at my ranch and Belle would have all the space she needs to run. She'll even have friends—I've got a couple border collies that work with the cattle."

She opened her mouth to argue that he had done more than enough already, that she couldn't continue to rely on him, but the words clogged in her throat.

The thought of being alone, of staying in that big, isolated house in the canyon, filled her with cold dread.

"I don't have anything. Clothes, pajamas. Nothing. I don't even have a leash for Belle." The staggering reality of all she had lost seemed suddenly too much to endure. Her eyes burned and she fought down a thick sob.

Wyatt seemed to sense her distress. He pulled her to him again and she let herself lean into his strength.

"She won't need a leash on my ranch, and you can wear something of mine tonight," he said. "I'll take you shopping for whatever you need tomorrow."

She needed *everything*. Just thinking about all she had to do—the myriad details necessary to rebuild a life—paralyzed her.

It was foolish to push aside his help, especially when she found the thought of having someone there to help her with the details—even to provide moral support—immensely comforting.

"All right. Thank you."

"Come on. Let's give Kirby a number where he can reach you, then we'll get you and Belle out of here."

Just this once, she promised herself, she could lean on him. She would worry about the danger to her heart later.

* * *

She was going to wring his sneaky neck, Taylor thought the next morning as she faced Wyatt across the sun-splashed Mexican tile of his kitchen work island.

"Your brother is getting married *here?* And you didn't think to mention this to me last night before dragging me up here?"

To his credit, he looked a little abashed. "Sorry. I guess it slipped my mind."

"You're having two hundred people here tomorrow and it *slipped your mind?*"

"You have to admit, I was a little busy, what with learning about police corruption and the death threats and your house burning up and all. It was a pretty full evening."

Oh, she was tired. Her eyes were as gritty and red as if she'd dumped a bucket of sand on her head, and her temples throbbed. How much stemmed from the traumatic events of the night before and how much was from her lack of sleep, Taylor couldn't say.

She hadn't been able to get through to Kate in Gualemala until the early hours of the morning. And though the guest room Wyatt showed her to was charming and comfortable, her mind had raced for hours before she had finally dropped into an exhausted sleep.

Maybe she would be dealing with this better if she wasn't so tired. "I can't stay here. Surely you see that. The last thing you need on your hands is a homeless, clothes-less, *everything*-less waif and her dog. I'll just open the cabin."

"Of course you can stay here. Why not? Lynn—my mother—and Gage's fiancée, Allie, are handling all the details for the wedding. As best man, all I have to do is take Gage out to try to get him good and sauced tonight, then show up in the monkey suit tomorrow. The rest of my time is free."

"I'm a stranger. I don't even know your family. They won't want me here at such an important family time!"

"I want you here and it's my house. As far as I'm concerned, that's all that matters."

Wyatt shrugged, so nonchalant, that she wanted to belt him. Could he really be so oblivious? Could he really not see how awkward and out of place she would be?

Wyatt went on. "Besides, my mother will adore you. She's always looking for a new cause. She'll take one look at you and your homeless dog and take to you like a honeybee to a petunia."

"I don't have anything to wear to a wedding." She heard the purely feminine whine in her voice and despised herself for it. She decided she despised him more when he only laughed and pulled her into his arms for a quick, unexpected hug.

"Have I mentioned how much I like that outfit you're wearing?" he murmured, a low note in his voice that sent shivers down her spine.

She grimaced and looked down at his T-shirt, which skimmed past her knees.

Her clothes had been ruined by the fire. They were soot-stained and smoky and she couldn't bear the idea of putting them on again, though she knew she would have to when they went shopping later.

She stepped away, needing the safety of a little distance from him. "Right. Like I'm going to show up at your older brother's wedding in a ratty T-shirt."

"Hey, I love that shirt."

"It shows, McKinnon."

He laughed and returned to the scrambled eggs he was stirring. "You won't have to wear it much longer. Mom and Allie are on their way over with some girlie stuff for you to borrow until we can go shopping."

"Right now?" She forgot all about her angst over the next day's wedding celebrations in the far more immediate trepidation of meeting his family so unexpectedly.

He nodded. "I called earlier this morning and explained the situation to my mother. She'll set you up with everything you need and then you and I can escape all the caterers and the decorators and the rest of the wedding craziness by running to Ogden to buy whatever else you need."

"Wyatt—" she began, but whatever argument she was trying to form flew out of her head as she heard a car pull up outside, then the excited chatter of high, female voices.

"That would be the troops." Wyatt smiled.

"Already?" Panic spurted through her. "I need some clothes. What will they think if they come in and find me like this?"

Wyatt looked her over, a strange, hot light in his eyes that made her stomach flutter.

"Probably that we've had a night of wild, steamy sex."

"We haven't!"

"I believe I'm aware of that," he said wryly, then grinned. "But then, if we had, you'd probably be a whole lot more relaxed right now."

She smacked him with the closest thing she could find, a dish towel patterned with chili peppers.

He laughed and grabbed it from her, then tugged her into his arms for a quick, heartbreakingly casual kiss. "Don't worry, Tay. They know what happened to your house last night. No one will give a second thought to how you're dressed."

A quick knock sounded at the door and Taylor scrambled away from him just as it opened and two little dark-haired girls bolted through.

"Hi, Uncle Wyatt." The older one hugged his leg. "Can I go ride your horsey?"

"Me too. Me too! I wanna ride Lucy," the other one exclaimed.

Taylor watched, charmed, as Wyatt picked one little girl up, kissed her forehead with a loud smack, then repeated the gesture with the other, amid a chorus of giggles.

"I don't think your mom would be too crazy about that plan today, girls. How about if we save it for next week while your mom and Gage are in San Francisco on their honeymoon? Tell Grandma Lynn to bring you over, okay?"

"Okay," the older of the two said with a heavy, put-upon sigh. Then she caught sight of Belle, lying in a pool of morning sunshine from the bay window.

"A dog! Look, Anna!" she exclaimed. "Uncle Wyatt has a new doggy!"

"Not mine," he corrected. "This is my friend, Taylor. Belle is her doggy."

The girls immediately rushed to Belle. Taylor stepped forward with concern, as Belle didn't have a great deal of experience with children, but she needn't have worried. The dog calmly endured the girls' excited attention. The older girl threw her arms around Belle's neck and hugged her tightly, but the dog only licked at her face, sending both girls off on another round of sweet giggles.

A moment later, two women came through the door, both carrying armloads of fall flowers in rich crimsons and yellows and umbers.

"Here, let me get some of those," Wyatt said, taking some from the older of the two and setting them on his dining table before returning to kiss each woman on the cheek in turn.

"Thank you, dear. There are more in the car. Would you mind grabbing them?"

This must be his mother, Taylor thought, mortified all over again at what she was wearing—or more precisely, what she wasn't wearing.

Lynn McKinnon was one of those women who had aged gracefully. With a son as old as Wyatt—and one older, Taylor remembered—she had to be at least in her late fifties but she looked a decade younger.

Taylor narrowed her gaze. Something about her lovely, warm features reminded her of someone, but she couldn't immediately place her. Perhaps she was only seeing the son in the mother.

The other woman, Wyatt's future sister-in-law, was blond and small and lovely. The smile she gave Taylor was open and friendly.

"Mom, Allie, this is Taylor Bradshaw," Wyatt said on his way out the door. "The friend I told you about. Taylor, this is my mother, Lynn McKinnon, and Alicia de Barillas, soon-to-be McKinnon. And the two rugrats are Gabriella and Anna."

Lynn McKinnon's eyes filled with compassion and, before Taylor realized her intent, she reached for Taylor's hands and gave them both a warm squeeze. "I am so sorry about your house," she said. "I was sick about it when Wyatt told me. Just sick. I'm so relieved my son was there with you so that you wouldn't have to be alone after such a horrible ordeal."

Taylor didn't know how to react to such warmth from her or the empathy in Allie's expression. These women didn't even know her! They had enough to worry about, with a wedding the next day.

"Thank you," she finally murmured.

"We brought you clothes and some makeup," Allie said.

"We didn't know your size for certain, but I think what we have will work for you."

"Thank you," she said again, overwhelmed. "I am so sorry to barge in on you like this in the middle of your wedding. If I had known, I never would have agreed to come. You have a million things to do besides worry about some stranger."

"Don't be silly," Lynn said. "You and Wyatt can go shopping for the things you need today and then tonight you must come over to my house. We're having a wild bachelorette party."

"Oh, no. I couldn't intrude."

"You wouldn't be intruding," Allie insisted with a smile. "We'd love to have you!"

"Grandma Lynn says we're all gonna pop popcorn and watch *Beauty and the Beast* on DVD," the girl named Gabriella said with excitement. "My favorite."

Taylor said with a smile, charmed by the girl and by the insight into just how "wild" the bachelorette party was likely to be.

"I love it too," Anna said with a wide, gap-toothed grin. "And we get to stay up until *ten-thirty!* Can you bring your doggy?"

"We'll have to figure that out," Lynn said. "Come on, Taylor. Let's see if any of the clothes we brought fit you."

Without giving her a chance to argue, Lynn grabbed her out of the kitchen, and Taylor discovered just where the son learned his high-handedness—and his kindness.

Chapter 9

With an exaggerated flourish, Wyatt twirled his mother around the dance floor that had been improvised on his broad deck overlooking the vast mountains.

Mother Nature had cooperated with a lovely fall day, sunny and mild with a brilliant blue, cloudless sky.

Allie and Gage had been married in a sweet, solemn ceremony in the same tiny chapel in Liberty where his mother—and all three of her children—had been christened.

Allie had cried, his mother had cried. Hell, he thought even Gage had shed a tear or two. After all the blubbering seemed to be through, the party had adjourned to his ranch.

The late-afternoon sun cast stretched-out shadows across his deck where a truly horrible band made up of Gage's FBI buddies was filling in while the regular musicians took a break.

At least the drummer could keep time, Wyatt thought with a grin as he and his mother two-stepped across the deck.

"I'd forgotten what a good dancer you were," Lynn said with a breathless laugh.

He dipped her low, then brought her vertical again with another elaborate flourish. "I'm a regular Fred Astaire. Who would ever guess I'm the same kid who spent a childhood constantly tripping over my own feet—as well as everyone else's."

She made a face at him. "Oh, stop. You weren't that bad."

"How many pairs of glasses do you think you bought me between the ages of seven and fifteen?"

"At least three a year."

She laughed and he thought how lovely she still was, even after all she had been through.

"I don't know who was more relieved when you finally switched to contact lenses—me, your optometrist or all the girls who could finally see those heartbreaking eyes of yours."

"Right. That was me, the gawky, skinny klutz with the heartbreaking eyes."

Lynn shook her head. "You were never as awkward as you seemed to think."

"Says my adoring mother."

He grinned, although the talk about his klutziness reminded him of the one terrible day he couldn't change, when it had mattered.

If he hadn't fallen off his bike just before Charlotte was kidnapped, perhaps he might have been able to see more than the color of a car so police could have sharpened their search for his sister.

He sobered at the reminder, then was angry at it. How long did they all have to suffer? Why did his sister's shadow have to blight this day that should be nothing but joy?

Would they ever have a day of full-on sunshine, without that shadow that always seemed to hover over them?

He sensed Lynn had been thinking of Charley too at various moments during the day. After twenty-odd years, he had learned to recognize that faraway look in her eyes, the tight set of her features.

She must have been thinking of her daughter—it would be extremely difficult at the marriage of one child not to wonder and worry about the one who was lost.

"Today was a good day, wasn't it?" he asked, compelled somehow to remind her.

Lynn smiled, though it was a little wobbly. "Perfect. Allie makes a lovely bride. Just what I have always dreamed of for Gage. She and her girls have been so wonderful for him."

Wyatt followed his mother's gaze to Gage and Allie. They were dancing together in the corner, and though Gage looked slightly unsteady on his legs, they both seemed radiantly happy.

He couldn't help thinking about the hard man Gage had been at the beginning of the summer. Testy and taciturn, he had pushed them all away at every turn.

Finding Allie and her girls had mellowed him, softened his hard edges. Wyatt was thrilled that Gage had found a woman who made him so happy—just as he was thrilled that because those edges had softened, Gage and their mother had begun to rebuild their relationship damaged by guilt and loss and pain.

Taylor suddenly whirled by him in the soft blue dress she had picked out the day before at a little boutique in Riverdale. She was on the arms of his father, who winked at Wyatt.

"This band stinks, doesn't it?" Sam asked, then didn't wait around for an answer before twirling her away.

"Dad looks good, don't you think?" he asked Lynn, then was surprised when she blushed and focused on a spot over his right shoulder.

"Your father always looks good," she murmured, then quickly changed the subject. "I like your friend Taylor very much."

Now it was his turn to feel uncomfortable. "Yeah. I like her too."

"We had a wonderful time at the party last night. We pigged out on popcorn and pizza and played games until the girls fell asleep, then the grown-up girls watched a chick flick. It was great." She smiled at him. "How long will she be staying?"

"That's up to her." He shrugged. "The invitation is open-ended. She hasn't figured out what she's going to do yet, but I know she's anxious to return to law school and the rest of her obligations in Salt Lake. Whatever she decides, I hope she takes at least a few more days here."

"Poor thing. How awful to lose her home like that, especially after all she and her family have been through. She told me you're helping her look into her brother's case. That's the case you're writing about now, isn't it?"

Right. The one he was losing all perspective about. He started to answer, but Sam and Taylor circled around to them again. This time Sam stopped by them as the song ended with a crash of discordant notes. To everyone's relief, the real musicians wrested their instruments back and immediately struck up an old Cole Porter love song.

"Aw, now this is more like it," Sam said with a smile. "Lynn, can I have the honor?"

Wyatt was amused—and a bit disconcerted—to see his mother blush again and slip willingly into her ex-husband's arms. On the plus side, it left him free to dance with Taylor.

He didn't want to think how perfect she seemed in his arms, tall and lithe and desirable. He *wouldn't* think about it, he decided. If he did, he was likely to embarrass both of them.

"You have a great family," she said.

Wyatt couldn't argue with that. "We have our problems but I wouldn't trade them."

"I believe I've danced with an uncle, a first cousin and a second cousin twice removed. And now your father."

"Both of my parents grew up around here," he said. "Throw a stick in town and you're likely to hit a relative of mine. Do you have extended family?"

"My father was an only child and I never knew my mother's family. I think she had an estranged sister but I don't remember ever hearing much about her." She made a face. "With both our parents gone, I only have Hunter left. It's a little tough to have family reunions in prison."

He squeezed her hand in sympathy and she sent him a sidelong look. "I sound like a baby, don't I? I'm sorry."

"You're trying to make the best of a tough situation."

"And not succeeding very well, usually." She paused, then made a transparent attempt to change the subject. "I like your house, Wyatt. There's a quiet here. A peace."

"Yeah. That's why I bought it. No matter whatever craziness I have to deal with on the outside, I can come here to find sanity and calm."

That peace seemed worlds away right now, with Taylor in his arms and the slow glide of the dance, he admitted to himself. She shouldn't fit there so perfectly. It only made his body ache more for her.

He was sure his palms must be sweaty, his movements as jerky and awkward as in those gawky teen years, but she didn't seem to notice. She swayed in his arms in time with a slow, sweet love song.

After a moment, she closed her eyes, savoring the music and the cool afternoon breeze ruffling her auburn hair.

He couldn't seem to push away the memory of kissing her

the week before in her office. He would swear he could still taste her on his lips, still feel her twisting those arms around his neck and drawing him closer.

The urge to kiss her almost overwhelmed him. He even caught himself leaning forward, his mouth eager to taste her again, but he managed to check the motion just in time, praying she didn't notice. The abrupt movement threw off his dance rhythm a little and he stumbled against her.

"Sorry," he murmured. "I'm a little out of practice."

At kissing and at dancing, he acknowledged ruefully. Both were dangerous activities to his equilibrium, especially where Taylor Bradshaw was involved.

The reception broke up soon after Wyatt's brother and his new wife drove away amid a shower of bubbles and sunflower seeds.

From the wide deck of his ranch house, Taylor watched the last guests drive away just as the sun slid behind the mountains. After the crowds and excitement of the afternoon, the ranch echoed with a silence broken only by the piercing cry of a hawk wheeling and diving overhead and the evening breeze moaning in the tops of the pine trees.

The air was sweet here, clear and scented with the sharp, citrusy tang of pine and fir. Inhaling it into her lungs brought back many happy memories of childhood weekend trips to their cabin in Little Cottonwood Canyon.

For all their conflicts, her father and brother shared a love of fishing. In the stream, they could at least try to find common ground. Taylor wasn't big on fishing but as long as she could take a book or two along, she hadn't minded the long days of solitude while Hunter and the Judge tried out woolly buggers and renegades.

Her stern, unapproachable father seemed to mellow on those trips. She supposed it was a little hard to stay solemn and dignified and judicial when he was traipsing through thick willows on the slippery riverbank wearing hip waders.

She let her mind pick through those pleasant memories while she automatically started to straighten some of the mess left by the wedding guests.

"You don't have to do that."

Wyatt's voice from the doorway startled her and she bobbled a glass and nearly dropped it. With an exclamation she reached for it just before it would have shattered on the deck.

"Nice save," he said with a grin as he walked out to join her under the dusky, orange-streaked sky.

She made a face. "I wasn't expecting you. I thought you were supposed to be changing your clothes."

"Doesn't take me long to climb out of the monkey suit. I see you've already changed."

"I don't have many nice clothes left. I need to take care of the ones I have until I have the chance to build up my wardrobe a little more."

"You don't have to do that," he repeated when she continued collecting napkins and plates. "The caterer and her people are taking care of the dishes and I've got a crew coming in the morning to clean the rest."

"I don't mind."

"I do. You need to work on relaxing, Ms. Bradshaw."

"I'm afraid I'm not very good at that."

"No kidding?" He grinned. "Since you've got a jacket, let's take a walk. We've still got a half hour or so of twilight—this is a gorgeous time to see my ranch. Come on, I'll show you my favorite spot."

She wasn't used to leisure time. For the past eight years

she'd been a student, always aware in the back of her mind there was something else she should be doing. Studying, working on a project, researching a report.

And then for the past two, every spare minute had been spent on Hunter's appeal. She *wasn't* very good at relaxing, but she decided now was as good a time as any to try.

They walked away from the house with its rock and log facade and charming gables, along a pathway that passed a barn and several outbuildings, all painted a traditional red. Belle followed him, along with Wyatt's two black-and-white border collies, Abbott and Costello.

It *was* a lovely evening. Not full dark yet—with the lavender glow of twilight making everything shimmer—the ranch seemed a magical place surrounded by soaring mountains. The air here smelled of fall, of dying leaves and distant woodsmoke.

They walked along a split-rail fence toward a copse of trees in a peaceful silence broken only by the dogs panting ahead of them and leaves crunching under their feet.

Even though the silence wasn't uncomfortable, Taylor was painfully aware of him. All day she had watched him interact with his family, dancing with his mother, talking quietly with his father, teasing his brother's new stepdaughters. She had found herself watching him far more often than was good for her.

Her awareness of him was only heightened by that dance they had shared. She hadn't been able to stop thinking about the strength of his arms around her.

As they neared the trees, she could hear the murmur of a small stream. The trees had camouflaged another red-painted outbuilding, a gazebo, about fifteen-feet square, with screened walls.

"Here it is. My holy sanctuary," Wyatt said when they reached the door. "I don't let very many people inside."

She couldn't contain her smile in response to the *solemn* gravity of his tone. "I'm honored."

"You should be."

Inside the door, he flipped a switch and low lights illuminated a comfortable outdoor room with a table and a few chairs, a refrigerator, even a plump couch facing the creek. It was more a self-contained sunroom than a gazebo, she realized now. The screen windows all around could be closed to keep out the elements for a year-round haven.

"This is wonderful! You could live out here."

"I'm tempted sometimes, believe me. I do my best work here by the creek. The great thing is that it's phone-free. Not even cell phones are allowed. Hard-and-fast rule."

"I'll remember that. I guess it's a good thing I left mine back in my room."

He smiled and leaned against the edge of the table. "I like to listen to the sound of the creek while I work. It's almost a Zen thing, like shifting to another level of consciousness. I can't explain it. I only know it does wonders for my powers of concentration. Here's one of your first lessons in relaxation. Sit down and just enjoy."

He turned the lights out again and Taylor obediently sat on the couch. She closed her eyes and let the ripple of the water and the sounds of twilight soothe her.

It might even have worked if Wyatt hadn't decided to sit beside her on the couch. Just how was she supposed to relax with him so close, filling her senses with his heat and the subtle, erotic scent of his cologne?

"Thank you for letting me share in your family's big day," she said after a moment.

"You were more than welcome. I hope you know that."

"Allie and Gage make a great couple. I know they'll be very happy together. They fit, somehow. That sounds silly, I guess."

He laughed softly. "Not so silly. I've thought the same thing. Allie is perfect for him. She won't take any of his garbage and she'll keep him from feeling like he has to take on the world."

"Do you and your brother get along?" she asked after a moment.

In the moonlight, he looked surprised at the question she had been wondering about all day. "Well enough, I guess. Why do you ask?"

She ought to have just kept her mouth shut. Feeling foolish, she tried to backtrack. "Nothing, really. A few times today I thought maybe I was picking up some strange undercurrents between the two of you, but I'm sure I must have been imagining things."

He was quiet for several moments, so quiet she thought perhaps he wasn't going to respond.

"No," he finally said. "You weren't imagining things. Gage and I have lived apart since we were kids. Our folks split up when I was ten and Gage was thirteen."

He was quiet again, and her heart ached at the pain in his voice that he wasn't quiet able to hide.

"After the divorce, Gage stayed with Dad in Las Vegas while I came home to Utah with Mom. We weren't estranged, we just led different lives as adults. I guess we're just getting to know each other again since Gage moved back."

She thought of Hunter, who had been her strength and her comfort through so many difficult times.

"You must have missed him a lot," she murmured.

"Yeah, I did." He paused. "I idolized Gage. He was my

older brother and I always thought he was stronger and faster and better than any other kid alive. To me, he was Evel Knievel, Superman and Muhammad Ali, all rolled up into one."

He laughed but the sound was without humor. "That first year after Mom and I moved back was miserable. I hated having my own bedroom. I didn't know what to do with myself. Gage and I had always shared a room—we were typical boys, fighting over whose turn it was to take out the garbage, whose side of the room was messier, who left the dirty towels on the bathroom floor. Until I was nine, we were your average family. Then, in a moment, everything changed."

Ah, here it was. The deep pain she had sensed running through this family. "What happened?" she asked quietly. "Does it have to do with your sister? Charlotte, isn't that her name?"

He tensed beside her like the sudden instinctive clenching of a fist at the first sign of danger. In the moonlight, she saw his jaw tighten, his eyes turn as dark and cloudy as a February night.

"I'm sorry," she said quickly, mortified at her nosiness. "Forget I asked. None of my business, obviously."

His words were low, rough. "After twenty-three years, hearing her name still always seems to knock me on my butt."

"I'm sorry," she said again. She scrambled for another topic—the weather? Allie's darling daughters?—but before she could form the words, he spoke in a flat, dispassionate voice that belied the emotion in his eyes.

"Charlotte was our little sister. When she was three years old, she was kidnapped from our front yard."

Taylor's instinctive gasp echoed through the gazebo. Kidnapped! Of all the grim scenarios she might have envisioned to explain their sister's absence from the family, that would never have occurred to her.

She might have thought the girl died after a tragic accident, or from a horrible disease—but a kidnapping? She couldn't even imagine it!

She couldn't think what to say, what to do. She longed to throw her arms around him, but he suddenly seemed as distant and unapproachable as the dark mountains silhouetted against the sky. She had to do something, though, so she settled for covering his hand with hers.

He turned his hand over and squeezed her fingers. "There are moments in life—in the tiniest flicker of a second—that completely change the course of your world. My life was forever altered in that instant Charley was kidnapped."

"What happened?" She didn't want to ask the question—wasn't sure she really wanted to know the answers—but on some deep, instinctive level she sensed he needed to talk about it.

He seemed lost in some nightmarish past she couldn't even imagine. "It was a hot August afternoon, another in an endless line of hot August afternoons that summer in Las Vegas. Mom went to the store for a moment to pick up a few things and left Gage and me in charge. Well, Gage, actually, but a friend wanted him to come over for a minute, so I was the one watching Charley when it happened."

He didn't say anything for several moments, gripping her hand so tightly her fingers throbbed.

"We were outside playing, even though it was so hot the sidewalks shimmered and the dry wind scorched your lungs. I had been trying all summer long to learn how to pop a wheelie on my bike like Gage could do, so I was practicing in the driveway, up and down, up and down. Charlotte was in the little grassy front yard running through the sprinkler that spurted up halfheartedly. I was too busy on my bike to pay her much attention."

He was a storyteller, she realized. He seemed compelled to paint her word-pictures, even with this grim story. Or maybe because of it. Maybe he had replayed these terrible events in his mind so many times, describing the scene to someone else seemed second nature.

"I had found minuscule success in my wheelie efforts, raising the tire maybe two inches off the ground, and I suppose I got a little cocky. I whipped my front tire up in the air one time a little harder than I had tried before and ended up crashing backward on the pavement. My glasses flew off, of course, and I can remember the sickening sound of them breaking. Seems like I spent half my life with broken glasses. I was trying to find them to see if I could piece them together when a car pulled into the driveway."

He closed his eyes. "I was blind as a bat without my glasses but I could tell it was a white car, the same color as Mom's station wagon. She was going to be so mad, I remember thinking, and I was so busy trying to think of an excuse for breaking my glasses for about the sixth time that summer that I barely registered the car pulling away again. I managed to hold a broken lens up to one eye long enough to figure out it wasn't Mom's station wagon, but I just thought maybe it was somebody turning around."

He opened his eyes and the stark pain in them sliced at her heart.

"It wasn't until the car had turned the corner that I realized Charley wasn't running through the sprinklers anymore."

"Oh, Wyatt."

He released her hand and rose to stand by the screened windows overlooking the creek. "Mom came home a few minutes later and called the police but I couldn't give them anything to go on, other than the color of the car. I was the only eyewitness and I was completely worthless."

A deep, terrible guilt threaded through his voice. Survivor's guilt. She had seen it often enough during her work at the hospital. His sister had been taken from right in front of him, so of course he would feel responsible. What a horrible burden for a nine-year-old!

"You were a child," she murmured.

"Yeah, but I was her big brother. I was supposed to stand between her and danger, and I didn't even know she was gone until it was too late."

Acting on instinct, she rose and followed him to the window and wrapped her arms around him, wishing she could somehow absorb this pain into her.

"I'm so sorry, Wyatt."

He stayed frozen for a moment as if he didn't quite know how to respond to her sympathy, and then his arms wrapped around her and he held her tightly. They stood that way for several moments in silence broken only by the tumble of water and the rustle of dry leaves in the wind.

"They never found her," he said finally, his chin resting on her head. "How could they, when they had nothing to go on?"

"How terrible for your parents. For all of you."

"The year after Charlotte disappeared seems surreal in my memory. We tried to go on with life—but how could we when such a huge, glaring chunk had been gnawed out of it? My parents' marriage disintegrated. They didn't fight in front of us, but I'm sure there was blame being flung around as we all tried to cope with her loss. If only Mom hadn't gone to the store. If only Dad hadn't moved us all to Vegas in the first place. A million if-onlys."

He was quiet again and she could hear each beat of his heart.

"They stayed together for a year, but I guess the strain became too much and they went their separate ways, each taking a son."

"And all these years you've found no trace of her?"

She felt his chin move against her hair as he shook his head. "Gage and I both follow a stray lead here or there, but the case has been cold for twenty-plus years. We haven't given up—I don't expect we'll ever give up—but realistically we all know the likelihood of ever finding her again is just about zero."

She stepped away from him though she still held tight to his hand. "That's why you write what you do, isn't it? 'I write for the victims and the victims' loved ones.' That's what you told that *Vanity Fair* reporter."

She remembered the rest of the quote. *"Though it doesn't take away any of their pain, victims' families deserve to know the truth about what happened and, more importantly, to know their lives won't be forgotten."*

She recalled wondering when she read his comments if he had lost someone. Now that she knew he had—now that she knew *him*—she hated knowing he had endured this pain.

"I wrote my first book about a serial kidnapper because I wanted—needed—to see inside his mind, to try to understand how someone can rip apart a family like that, destroy lives, shatter dreams, without a single qualm. I guess with every book I write I'm trying to answer that question. I don't think I ever will."

She curled her fingers around his. "I'm glad you and Gage have reestablished your relationship. You shouldn't have to lose a brother too because of what happened to your sister."

"I don't tell many people about Charlotte. I'm not sure why I told you—maybe because for all the joy today with Gage's wedding, I seem to feel her absence most acutely at special occasions like this. I think we all do."

"That's only natural. I'm sure it was a hard day for your parents too."

"Thank you for listening. You do it well. A good trait for a doctor to have."

"I'm not a doctor," she reminded him.

"You should be."

She shook her head, frustrated at his insistence, so much like Hunter's, but it still made her smile.

He gazed at her in the moonlight and something in his expression made her breathless, made her insides shiver.

Chapter 10

Later, she wasn't certain who made the first move. She might have tugged him to her or he may have reached out. Either way, an instant later she was in his arms again and his mouth descended to hers.

In the chill of the autumn evening, his lips were seductively warm—enticing, welcoming. She wanted to curl up against him, settle in right here for the night while the cool air eddied around them and the stream bubbled and sang.

Ah, heaven.

When the rest of her life seemed so chaotic, as discordant as that music the temporary band had tortured them all with earlier, how could she manage to feel such peace here in his arms? Despite the race of her blood and the tremble of need inside her, her heart seemed to settle, her wild turmoil of thoughts to still.

She had known him—*really* known him—only a few

weeks. It seemed far longer. Only a few short weeks ago she had thought he was an opportunistic writer out to make a buck off the suffering of others.

How could she have misjudged him so completely?

The Wyatt she had come to know was so different from the man she had thought him. He was good and kind, passionate about his work and his family—a family that had suffered deep pain.

He had more layers than she ever would have guessed.

"I haven't been able to stop thinking about this since the first time we kissed," he murmured against her mouth.

A lifetime ago, she thought. So much had happened since then. That first kiss in her office had been purely physical, an outlet for the attraction she hadn't wanted to acknowledge. She knew him so much better now—and like Wyatt himself, her response to this kiss was layered with nuances.

She was still fiercely attracted to him—even more than she'd been before. But now she was attracted not just to a lean, sexy man but to the man who teased his new nieces and danced with his mother and welcomed Taylor into his family as if she belonged there.

She poured all of that and more into her response, and he kissed her with the same heat.

As his mouth explored hers, tenderness welled inside her, bubbling through her like that stream outside their sanctuary. She shivered at the strength of it—and at the terrifying realization that her heart was in far more jeopardy than she ever would have believed.

Though the movement was slight, Wyatt sensed the fine tremble of her muscles. "You're cold," he murmured.

"No. Trust me, I'm not cold."

Her voice sounded rough, thready, and it skated down his nerve endings like a soft caress. He responded by slipping his hands inside her jacket to her waist where the shirt she wore allowed him easy access to the soft skin above the waistband of her jeans. "You're right. You're not cold. "

"And you're not even close to the really hot parts."

Oh, but he wanted to be. Wanted it so fiercely he suddenly couldn't seem to breathe.

Lauding whatever instinct had prompted him to install a comfortable couch in his writing retreat, he lowered her to the couch, stretching out above her. Those incredibly long legs slid apart slightly, welcoming him, and he nearly groaned at the tumult of sensations cascading through him.

From the first touch of their mouths he had been aroused, hard and heavy, and even through their thick clothing, his body cried out to hers. He wanted her right here, right now.

He slid his hands from her waistband to her high breasts, touching her through the cotton of her shirt. She arched against him with a low, aroused sound and he deepened the kiss.

An instant later Wyatt heard the mournful hoot of the owl that lived in tree along the river and the sound seemed to jar him back into his senses like a warning.

What the hell was he doing? If he didn't put the brakes on things right now, they would both be naked and he would be inside her before either of them knew what happened.

He had to put a stop to things now, while he still had a tiny sliver of strength remaining.

Seducing her had never been his intention when he invited her to take a walk with him. He knew having her in his house would be a supreme test of willpower but he had vowed, even as he invited her to stay, that he would not take advantage of the situation.

She had been through so much this last week. The threat and then the fire at her house. For her sake, he couldn't complicate things further by throwing intimacy into the mix. It wouldn't be fair, not when their emotions were so close to the surface.

He wasn't concerned only about her, he acknowledged. *He* was in trouble here.

The thought seemed to echo through his mind like that owl's cry. Taylor Bradshaw posed a serious threat to his peace of mind. He didn't like the protective impulses she drew out in him, the way she sneaked under his skin, the way he wanted to breathe her scent of rain-washed wildflowers into his lungs, absorb it into his soul.

Though it was the hardest thing he'd ever done and he prayed to heaven she couldn't see his hands tremble, he stood up, adjusting her clothes again and stepped away from the couch.

"We'd better go back inside and see how the caterers are coming with the wedding cleanup."

The moonlight cast enough glow that he couldn't miss the baffled hurt in her eyes or the flush that climbed her cheekbones. He wanted to explain that he was trying to protect both of them, but she rose from the couch and walked out into the night before he could find the words.

She was running away.

Maybe it was rationalizing but she preferred to look at it not as the act of a coward but as self-preservation.

Taylor loaded the last shopping bag into the back of her Subaru, then turned to whistle to Belle, who was saying her goodbyes to Wyatt's border collies, circling and sniffing one last time.

It was a gorgeous morning, crisp and clear with just the hint of a breeze. Though the sun hadn't completely cleared the mountains yet, she could tell it would be a beautiful day, the kind of Sunday perfect for a good brisk walk through the backcountry.

The air smelled sweet and clean and Taylor indulged herself for a moment just breathing it into her lungs. A pair of horses raced through a pasture at the base of the driveway, mane and tail catching the early morning sunlight, and she felt a pang at having to leave this beautiful ranch.

She had no choice, though. She couldn't stay here. There was too much at stake to risk it. She needed time and distance to rebuild the defenses that had shattered the night before in his arms.

No, they had shattered long before that, she acknowledged. She had been careless about protecting herself from hurt. Somehow when she wasn't looking, Wyatt McKinnon had mounted a sneak attack and she was still reeling from it.

"Come on, sweetie. Let's go," she ordered more firmly, and the dog snuffled reluctantly but clambered into the back seat.

Taylor opened the driver's door but before she could climb in she heard the squeak of the front door and turned to find Wyatt striding out onto the porch.

His hair was damp as if he had just stepped out of the shower and he wore faded jeans and a polo shirt that stretched across his muscles. She swallowed hard, wishing she could have made her escape five minutes earlier and avoided this encounter.

"You're off early."

She hated this defensiveness, especially as she knew how rude and ungrateful she must seem by her departure.

"Yes. I left you a note on the table. I appreciate all you've done. You and your family have been more than kind to me but I've got hours' worth of work to do to open up the cabin in Little Cottonwood Canyon and to catch up with course work. I thought an early start would be best."

"Why do you need to open the cabin? You're welcome to stay here as long as you need."

That would be a nightmare, staying here day in and day out and trying to pretend she wasn't developing feelings for him that terrified her.

"It's at least an hour commute from here to the university. I can cut that substantially by using my family's home."

"I don't like the idea of you being up there alone. Did you forget that threatening note—not to mention the minor little detail that someone just burned down your house?"

She blew out a breath. "I haven't forgotten. How could I? But I won't hide away up here with you. Whoever is doing all this wants me to cower and cringe and forget about helping Hunter. I can't. Anyway, I won't be alone for long. Kate is cutting her trip short and should be back by Tuesday. In the meantime, I'll have Belle. She'll be a good watchdog."

"I still don't like it. Look, I told you I have an apartment in Salt Lake I use when I'm traveling or working late in the city. It's only a few minutes from the university. Just use that. At least you would have neighbors around in an emergency."

The offer was tempting. She had to admit she still wasn't thrilled about staying at the cabin alone, even for the few days until Kate's return. But staying at his apartment wasn't so very different from staying here at the ranch. It would only be another thread between them that she would eventually have to snip.

"There are other year-round homes close to the cabin," she answered. "I'll be fine."

"Taylor—"

She cut him off. "Thank you again for rescuing Belle and for everything else these past few days." She didn't want to argue with him—nor did she want to remind him that he had no say in the matter.

His mouth—that wonderful, sensuous mouth that she knew entirely too well—tightened into a hard line. "Nothing I say will change your mind, will it?"

"I know you're concerned and I appreciate it, but I'll be fine. Don't worry about me."

"Right. You're walking completely unprotected back into what could be an extremely dangerous situation and you expect me to just sit back and accept it."

Why did he sound so angry? The man ought to be doing cartwheels to see her taillights in the distance! She had dragged him into this mess, had cried all over him, had invaded his home and his brother's wedding, for heaven's sake.

She did appreciate his help—and she was honest enough to admit she had desperately needed the time he offered her to cope with the trauma of losing her home and her belongings. But now she needed to return to the business of real life—before she was left forever scarred.

He went on. "Somebody torched your house, Taylor. What do you think his next step will be?"

She swallowed down a tremor of fear. "I don't know. Maybe the bastard will get careless and show himself so that I can prove who really killed Dru and Mickie."

"That knowledge is not going to do your brother or anybody else a whole hell of a lot of good if you're dead."

"I'll be fine," she repeated, wishing she could believe it herself.

A muscle worked in his jaw, and by the ferocity of his features, she had the feeling he would be more than capable of wresting her from the car and locking her in one of his guest rooms.

For one charged second, he gazed at her, then he growled a low, pungent oath. "I want to hear from you every day, understand? Every day. If I don't get a phone call, I'm coming to get you and drag you back here."

She nodded tightly.

He studied her for another moment, then pulled her to him for one swift, devastating kiss. "Be careful," he murmured.

She didn't trust herself to speak, so she only nodded again and slid behind the wheel. As she drove down the long, winding driveway of his ranch, she saw him in the rearview mirror, watching after her.

Be careful, he had said. She was terribly afraid it was far too late for that.

At least where her heart was concerned.

Three days later, Taylor sat in the university law library poring over citations for her civil procedure class. This was the hardest part of law school for her. She didn't mind the work, didn't mind researching old cases. Parts of it, she had to admit, she actually found interesting.

But the sometimes dry isolation of it bothered her. During her med school days, it seemed she was always surrounded by people. Professors, other students. Doctors, nurses, patients. She disliked sitting here alone with only her law books for company.

"Hey, Taylor. I finally found that docket number you were looking for earlier."

Grateful for the interruption, she glanced up to find Barbara Langley standing by her carrel. In her late fifties, with striking salt-and-pepper hair and a warm smile, Barbara was Taylor's favorite librarian. Unlike some of the others, she gave her help generously and enthusiastically.

"Thank you!" she exclaimed. In the chaos of the past few weeks, she had forgotten she had even asked the librarian earlier in the month. "This will be a big help."

"Is it for one of your classes or for your brother's appeal?"

Taylor stared at her, nonplussed. She had known Barbara for a year, since her terrible early months as a first-year, but this was the first time the librarian had made reference to Hunter. Had she known all along that Taylor was his sister?

She wasn't ashamed of her brother—far from it—but while her connection to him wasn't a secret, she tried not to advertise it. Things seemed easier that way, especially as she didn't enjoy answering unwanted questions. And the questions inevitably came. Hunter was almost as infamous in Utah as another native son, Butch Cassidy.

"Both, I guess," she said, answering the librarian's question. "I thought it might be on point for a paper I'm doing in my evidence class but I was also interested in its relevance to Hunter's case."

Barbara smiled and handed her the paper. "I hope you find what you're looking for."

She started to walk away, paused for a moment as if trying to make up her mind about something, then turned back to Taylor. "I should probably tell you, I followed your brother's trial closely."

Taylor held her breath. This was the point where people usually looked at her like she was next of kin to the devil himself.

Barbara's expression didn't change from her usual pleasant smile, though. "I'm not usually a trial junkie but I was interested in it mainly because I knew Mickie Wallace-Ferrin when she was plain old Mickie Wallace, struggling law student."

"Why haven't you said anything before?"

Barbara shrugged. "I figured if you wanted to talk about your brother's case you would have brought it up."

Taylor thought of those terrible days of the well-publicized court proceedings when she couldn't seem to walk into the grocery store without having to listen to trial commentary given by everyone from the produce manager to the bag boy.

"You know, Mickie was in here just a few weeks before she was murdered," Barbara said.

The information surprised her. Mickie hadn't been in good health for weeks before her death. Why would she have dragged herself out of her deathbed to the university law library?

"She looked awful. The poor woman could hardly walk and looked as if she would fall over if somebody so much as coughed in her direction, but she seemed mighty determined. For two hours she barely looked up from the cite she was studying."

"Do you remember the case?" Taylor asked, intrigued.

Barbara looked vaguely affronted. "Of course I do! How could I not? It was one of the most terrible murder cases the state has ever seen. *State of Utah v. Martinez.* I think it was 1974 or '75. Long before your time, of course. I started in 1972 and I'd only been here a few years when it happened. I do remember that Mickie was in for the prosecutor's office at the time and worked on the case."

Taylor frowned. "Why would Mickie want to scour through thirty-year-old case files? The woman was dying. I would think she'd have better things to do with her time remaining on earth."

"Beats me. Maybe she was reliving past victories. As I recall, the jury only took an hour or so to render a guilty verdict, and this was a death-penalty case like your brother's."

Her voice trailed off and her attention fixed on something over Taylor's shoulder. Barbara gave an appreciative smile wide enough that Taylor had no choice but to turn around and see what had caught her attention.

Her mouth went as dry as the humidity controlled air in the library and her train of thought completely derailed when she saw Wyatt approaching the table.

He wore tan Dockers, a slate-blue sweater and a leather jacket and he looked so gorgeous for a moment, all she could do was stare.

Though he hadn't been out of her mind for long, she hadn't seen him since that morning at his ranch four days earlier. As he had so sternly ordered, she had called him every day to check in, but she had kept her side of the conversation quick and impersonal.

The night before, he had reminded her on the phone that he was coming to the city and had insisted on meeting her for lunch, but she had thought she had at least another half hour to work.

With effort, she tried to kick-start her brain again and by the time he reached them, she almost thought she could string together a complete sentence.

"Wyatt! I thought we were meeting at the Broiler."

"I had some time after my interview and thought I'd come find you, see how things have been going."

Taylor glanced at Barbara and realized the librarian was looking on avidly. She was about to introduce them when Wyatt stepped forward and kissed the librarian's cheek warmly.

"How are you, Barb? I still owe you those Jazz tickets

for all the help you gave me on *Blood Feud*. I haven't forgotten, I promise. I just need to know what game you want to see."

"Jazz–Lakers, of course. Who else?"

He laughed. "Deal. I'll get them to you by the end of the week."

"My grandson loves basketball," Barbara explained to Taylor. "We go every chance we get."

She was embarrassed to realize she hadn't even known the woman had a grandson, let alone that she was a basketball fan—and yet Wyatt knew. She had figured out that he was the type of man who observed people around him, who tried to find out their likes and dislikes.

"I'd better get back to work," Barbara said to them both, then to Taylor she added, "Let me know if you need any more help."

"Thank you for this," Taylor said.

"I talked to the fire marshal this morning," Wyatt said after the librarian walked away. "He said he talked to you last night about the contents of his report."

She nodded grimly. "Definitely arson. The fire was started with gasoline, just as he suspected last week. It probably ignited only moments before we arrived."

"Any suspects?"

"Nothing concrete. He wondered if it might be the same serial arsonist who torched houses across the valley all summer, but the pattern on this one was different."

She hated knowing there was some unknown threat out there, some nameless faceless person she couldn't even identify who had such malice toward her that he would burn down her house. She felt helpless, terrified.

"Did your roommate make it back into the country?"

"Yes. I picked her up last night." She fidgeted with the strap of her bag. "In fact, I hope you don't mind but I invited her to lunch. She's meeting us at the restaurant."

Taylor didn't add that she had to beg Kate to join them. She hadn't been able to face the idea of spending time alone with Wyatt, not when her emotions were so raw. She needed a buffer between them, and Kate had reluctantly agreed.

If Wyatt was surprised by the unexpected addition to their lunch plans, he didn't show it. "Great. I look forward to meeting her. It's beautiful outside—why don't we walk?"

Taylor decided she could use some fresh air after being cooped up in class and the library all morning—not to mention that she wasn't looking forward to sharing the close confines of a vehicle with him.

"Great," she answered. "I just need to put these books upstairs in my carrel."

Wyatt followed her to her study desk on the second floor. He had used the law library enough while researching his books that he knew second- and third-year law students were assigned their own study carrels in the library or the connected law building.

Some students personalized their small study desk with cartoons and sayings, favorite photographs, funny little knick-knacks or even their own leather chairs.

Taylor's had nothing but a calendar and a half-dozen law books locked into the glass-fronted bookcase above the desk.

She quickly added the books she'd been reading to the others in the cabinet, slipped on a suede jacket that had been hanging over the back of a plain wooden chair, then followed him outside into the fall afternoon.

Rain the night before had left everything fresh and clean, and Wyatt watched her inhale deeply as if she'd been a prisoner in an airless dungeon for days.

She looked far too pale, as if she hadn't spent nearly enough time outside, and he wanted to pick her up, stuff her into his Tahoe and take her back to his ranch for a week or two until her skin lost that pallor.

He had missed her these past few days. He didn't like thinking about how much—how anxiously—he waited for her brief, stilted phone call each night.

Every day, it was all he could do to keep from driving down here and dragging her home with him, where she would be safe. He didn't realize just how worried he had been for her until he walked into that library. The wave of relief that had washed over him—and of tenderness, he acknowledged grimly—had just about knocked him to his knees.

It didn't take them long to walk to Market Street Broiler, just a block from campus. The restaurant was busy as usual, with a bustling lunchtime crowd.

Market Street and its downtown sister served the best seafood along the Wasatch Front and was perennially crowded. Wyatt asked for an upstairs booth, a request granted immediately by a friendly hostess.

"Kate said she might be a little late," Taylor said when they were settled at a table. "She had some things to do at the hospital this morning and wasn't sure exactly when she could get away."

She said the words with no bitterness, but still he wondered if it bothered her, watching her friend live the life he knew Taylor wanted.

He thought of her study carrel, dry and lifeless. That's what she would become if she continued on this course. Somehow he needed to work harder to help her find the truth about the murders, so she could stop this senseless self-sacrifice.

"My interview this morning was with a cousin and close

friend of Dru's, Candy Wallace," he said when they were seated.

"I think I saw her at the trial. How did it go?"

"It took a little prodding but Candy finally admitted Dru had confided in her that the baby's father was a married Salt Lake City cop."

Taylor's features lit up. "Just as we thought! Did Candy know his name?"

"Nothing concrete. She only heard Dru ever use his first name—John—so that's all she knows."

The animation on her features turned to dismay. "There must be a dozen men on the police force with that first name. Even Hunter's partner, John Randall."

Wyatt knew that in law enforcement, no one knew a man's strengths and weaknesses better than his partner. If someone wanted to twist evidence to make an innocent man look guilty, his partner would certainly know what would do the trick.

"It's not much," he said about the new information from his interview, "but at least it's a starting point."

"You know, right before you arrived at the library, Barbara was telling me that a few weeks prior to her death, Mickie spent time at the library reading up on an old murder case. According to Barbara, it was a case Mickie worked early in her career with the county prosecutor's office."

"Oh?"

"I wonder why she would care about some old case when she was dying," Taylor said, and Wyatt could almost see the wheels turning in that bright mind of hers.

"You know," she continued, "everybody always assumed Dru was the primary target and Mickie was just collateral damage. That's why the investigation turned so quickly to Hunter—the jealous, cukolded boyfriend. What if the police were wrong and it was the other way around? What if Mickie was the target all along?"

"How do you make that kind of jump just from Mickie looking up details of an old case?"

"I don't know. It just seems so odd to me. At this point I think I'm just grasping at straws."

"I guess you'll keep grasping until you pull out the right one or until you run out of straws."

"At least until Hunter is free." She paused, her gaze on the stairs. "Oh, here comes Kate."

Taylor slid across the booth seat to make room for her friend, and Wyatt stood as a petite blond woman joined them. He offered a welcoming smile that froze on his face when he caught sight of her features.

She had big blue eyes, a slender nose and a generous mouth that tilted up at the corners. Kate Spencer was a lovely woman, the kind of small, graceful creature that automatically made a man feel protective, want to tuck her close and keep her safe.

He felt as if someone had just karate-chopped him in the forehead, sending all his thoughts scattering, and for several seconds he couldn't seem to grab hold of a single one.

"Sorry I'm late," she was saying.

He thought maybe she added something else about not being able to find a parking space, but he could barely hear her over the buzzing in his ears.

Kate Spencer was a beautiful woman.

She was also the spitting image of his mother.

Chapter 11

"I'm delighted to finally meet you," Kate said, holding out her hand.

Wyatt could barely breathe. *Could it be? Was she Charlotte?*

He thought he must have managed to mumble some response. When he took her hand, he wanted to feel some shock of recognition, some surge of blood toward blood. Instead, he only felt a small, competent hand in his. He yearned to hang on to it, but good manners and societal expectations forced him to release it.

To his relief, the white-aproned waiter arrived just then, giving Wyatt much-needed time to scramble for his composure.

It *couldn't* be Charlotte. The odds against it were astronomical—that after all their years of searching—after all the dead ends and false hopes—he would just happen to bump into his abducted sister at lunch one day while he was going about the business of his life.

But, good lord! She looked exactly like pictures he'd seen of his mother on her wedding day, right down to the same tiny mole just under her left cheekbone.

Her eyes were just like Lynn's, that same crystal blue, and even her smile was the same—warm, open, a little mischievous.

A few years ago, Gage had hired a specialist to create an age-progressed image of what Charlotte might look like today. Wyatt had memorized that picture. As he compared it in his mind to the woman in front of him, he thought maybe the artist's rendering was a little off on the nose and Kate's hair color was perhaps a darker blond, but Wyatt was willing to bet if he held Gage's picture up right now to the woman sitting across from him, it would be dead-on.

"Wyatt?" Taylor's voice jerked him back to the table and he realized the server was waiting to take his order. "Um, I'll have whatever the special is today with chowder," he mumbled.

The waiter nodded and hurried away, leaving an awkward silence at the table.

He caught himself staring at Kate, looking for any clue that this wild hope surging through him might be justified.

"So Taylor tells me you're a doctor," he said, compelled to find out more about her.

He didn't miss the quick look she sent Taylor. "Yes. I'm a second-year intern at the University Hospital. Family medicine."

He couldn't seem to look away. He was aware of it, knew how odd it must appear to Taylor and Kate, but couldn't help it.

He wanted so much to reach across the table and pull her into his arms, but he knew he couldn't. Not yet. What if he was wrong? What if her uncanny resemblance to his mother was just some cosmic joke, an extraordinary coincidence.

He had to approach this all scientifically, try to dig into her past a little and find some verification before he did anything rash like declare to Kate that she could be his long-lost sister.

How would Gage handle this? He tried to think of his brother's methodical approach. A DNA test would be the logical first step, but how the hell could he pull that off?

No, the first step would be information-gathering, he decided, to find out as much about her as possible.

"Are you from Utah?"

Some of the friendliness on her face dimmed a little. "No. I grew up in Florida."

Florida! If she was Charlotte, how in heaven's name did she get from Las Vegas to Florida. "What part?"

"Various places. I lived in the Pensacola area the longest, from around age twelve to when I left home for college."

"Did you have a parent in the military? Is that why you moved around so much?"

She started to look a little uncomfortable at his probing. "Nope," she said, her voice almost short.

She didn't like talking about herself, he realized when she quickly changed the subject.

"How's the book business? Has Taylor convinced you of Hunter's innocence yet?"

He blinked at the frontal attack, then almost laughed, remembering how little Charley used to give as well as she got.

"I'm still withholding judgment," he said, although he wasn't sure if that was the truth. "I will say, there are more unanswered questions in this case than in any other I've written about."

"I enjoy your books," Kate said. "I read them even before Taylor found out you were writing about Hunter's case."

"It was Kate's idea to show you the new evidence I've found since the trial," Taylor said. "She read your books and knew you would be fair."

"I'm trying," he answered.

He had a million questions he wanted to ask this woman who looked so much like his mother, but the waiter's arrival with their chowder forestalled him. No worries, he thought, excitement pulsing through him. His questions could wait a little longer—unlike the Charlotte he had spent twenty-three years seeking, he knew just where to find Kate Spencer.

Taylor supposed she should be used to this by now, to men completely going mental over Kate. In the five years they had been first friends, then roommates, she'd seen it happen dozens of times. Taylor had seen men forget their own names when Kate smiled at them.

She might have seen it all before, but she had never experienced this crushing misery. Just a few days ago she had been wrapped in his arms, his mouth warm and hard on hers and his eyes filled with what she could have sworn was tenderness.

How could he turn so quickly to Kate?

She pushed away her uneaten pasta, wondering if this interminable meal would ever end.

At least Wyatt's interrogation of Kate about her life in Florida seemed to have stopped. Taylor was glad—she knew how much Kate disliked talking about her grim journey through the foster-care system or about the woman who had abandoned her to it.

She much preferred to focus on the kind foster parents who had taken her in from the age of twelve, who had loved her and mentored her and whose name she had finally taken when she reached adulthood and could make that choice for herself.

Why did it bother her so much, watching Wyatt lose his head over Kate? It wasn't as if she had any kind of claim on him. Despite his many kindnesses to her, he had made it abundantly clear the other night that while he might enjoy kissing her, he drew the line at anything further.

The answer hit her with a jolting shock, as if someone had just dumped their carafe of ice water on her head.

It bothered her so much—sliced at her heart like a dull razor—because she was falling in love with him.

How in the world could she have allowed such a disastrous thing to happen?

And now that she realized it, what was she going to do about it?

She was destined for heartbreak. Taylor recognized that unalterable fact with terrible clarity. There was no other outcome, no happy ending in it for her.

He cared about her—he wouldn't have insisted on those daily check-ins if he didn't—and he might have been temporarily attracted to her enough to kiss her a few times. But he wasn't in love with her and she couldn't compound her mistake by pretending otherwise.

"I'd better return to the hospital," Kate said after she finished her entrée.

She stood to go, and Taylor realized her roommate was just as relieved to have this meal over.

"Working?" Taylor asked. "You weren't even supposed to be back in the country until next week! How can you be on the schedule?"

"They were shorthanded so I offered to pull a shift. I can't turn down the money right now."

Guilt swamped her. Kate needed the money because, like Taylor, she had to replace everything she had lost in the fire. Until Taylor's homeowners' insurance came through, they would have to pay their own replacement costs for necessary items.

Kate was a struggling resident. Unlike Taylor, who had a

trust fund to fall back on if necessary, Kate often found money tight. Taylor had tried to give her a temporary loan until the insurance payment came through, but with typical Kate stubbornness, her friend had refused.

The fire was Taylor's fault. Whoever set it had been targeting her, had been trying to distract her from Hunter's appeal. She tried to explain that to Kate, but she wouldn't listen.

Taylor would figure out a way to make things right with her roommate, she vowed after Kate left—despite this ache in her heart that the man she loved was now apparently enamored with her.

"I know you're on your honeymoon. I'm sorry," Wyatt said into the phone fifteen minutes after he walked an uncharacteristically taciturn Taylor back to campus. "I would never have bugged you if it wasn't important, I swear."

"It damn well better be," Gage growled.

He held his breath, not sure how to spring the news on his brother.

"I think I've found her," he finally just blurted out, unable to hold back his growing excitement.

There was a long pause on the other end, then he heard muffled voices as Gage told Allie who he was talking to.

"I need you to use your Bureau connections to push through a DNA test," he said when his brother came back on the line. "Do you think you can put a rush on it?"

"Wait a minute. Slow down. Why do you think it's her?" Gage didn't bother asking who Wyatt was talking about—but then, Wyatt wouldn't have expected him to.

"Instinct. That's all I've got. Not much, I know, but when you see her, though you'll know what I mean. I'm telling you,

Gage, she looks just like Mom at that age—same eyes, same hair color, everything."

"Did you ask her about her past? For all you know she has six brothers and sisters who look just like her."

"She's an only child, raised in foster care in Florida. She has no siblings—or none she knows about yet."

"And you just happened to run into her and say, 'Hey, I think you might be my younger sister'?"

"No. I didn't say a word. It was the hardest damn thing I've ever had to do to keep my mouth shut. I don't know how it can be possible—where she's been all this time—but it has to be her."

"Odds are good that it's not."

He heard the warning in Gage's voice and had to admit to a great feeling of comfort at it. Gage was worried he would get his hopes dashed. Not this time, he thought. This time was real, he was positive.

"Wait until you see her," he responded.

"If you didn't say anything to her about Charlotte, how did you plan to get a sample for the DNA test?"

Wyatt grinned and eyed the doggy bag he'd carried out of the restaurant, along with the contents he had surreptitiously pilfered. "I think I've got it taken care of. I took her drinking straw. There should be enough DNA on it to run a test. So how soon can you arrange it? I'll give a blood test for comparison or whatever you need."

"I'm on my honeymoon!"

Right. He winced, wondering just how mad Allie would be at him for interrupting. Because of the girls and Gage's work commitments, they had only been able to squeeze out less than a week at a private, very exclusive escape along the Oregon Coast.

"Just give me the name of a lab you trust and I'll take care of everything," Wyatt said.

"No. I can make a few calls to expedite things. I'll let you know where to go from here."

"Why the hell didn't you tell me your house burned down?"

Taylor winced at her brother's angry voice ringing in her ear. He didn't give her any kind of greeting once she accepted the collect charges for his call to her cell phone from prison—he just started in on her.

She hitched up her bag but didn't ease her pace across campus. "How did you find out?"

"Does it matter?"

Yes, it mattered. She had purposely omitted that little tidbit of information from her conversation during her last visit with her brother. How would he have heard about it?

"Did Wyatt tell you?" she asked. She tried to stir up anger for him but she didn't know if she could find room in her heart to be mad, not with all the hurt stuffed in there.

"McKinnon? No. I haven't seen him for a while. Martin was here yesterday talking about the appeal. He mentioned your little fire in passing, assuming I knew all about it."

Drat the man. Martin had time to run to the prison telling tales but he didn't have time to talk to her about the appeal.

"Why didn't you tell me?" Hunter pressed.

"I didn't want you to worry," she admitted. "It was no big deal, really."

"Martin seemed to think otherwise. He's worried about you."

"I can take care of myself. He should be worrying about you."

She heard the heavy silence on the other end and braced herself for Hunter's protective big-brother routine. When he spoke, his voice was tired but firm.

"Enough is enough, Tay. I want you to go back to med school now. Today. Leave the appeal to Martin."

She sighed. Hadn't they been through this about a couple hundred times before? "I can't do that, Hunter. You know I can't. I have to try."

"It's not worth your life! What if you had been inside the house at the time?"

"I wasn't. I was with Wyatt. We were talking to a police sergeant about a story Dru was working on when she was killed, about deep police corruption in the department. We've made progress, Hunter. I can feel it."

"None of that matters if you're dead, Tay. Stop now."

"Don't you get it? If I stop I'll give whatever bastard did this to Dru and Mickie—to you—just what he wants. He'll get away with it. That's why the threat, why my house was set on fire. So I'll run scared and stop trying to find the truth."

"What threat?"

Rats. She hadn't meant to mention that little detail. "Nothing. Just a silly message. Drop it or else. That kind of thing."

"Did you go to the police?"

"I don't trust the police. Not anymore."

"There are still good people on the force, Tay."

"Maybe," she answered. "But right now I'm having a tough time figuring out the bad from the good. Did you know the father of Dru's baby was a married cop?"

He was quiet for a long time. "Yeah. I did."

An odd note in his voice caught her attention. "Do you know who it was?"

He didn't answer, which she considered a damning admission. "You know. I can tell you know. Who was he?"

"It doesn't matter now."

"Maybe it does! Think about it, Hunt. A married cop would

have one heck of a motive to kill Dru if she was threatening to go to his wife about their child. He would have the motive and his job would give him the means to pin it on you."

"He didn't kill her."

"You don't know that for sure! Tell me his name. Wyatt found out from Dru's cousin that his first name is John. The only John I know personally on the force is John Randall and I know it couldn't be him."

This time the silence was longer and Taylor gripped the phone tightly. It couldn't be. John Randall had been Hunter's best friend. A family man, a churchgoing man. How could he have cheated both his wife and his partner by carrying on an affair with the woman Hunter thought he loved?

John Randall had been one of the few cops to stand by Hunter during the trial, she remembered. Had Hunter known then that he was the baby's father?

"How long have you known it was John?" she asked.

Her brother sighed. "He came to see me during the trial and told me. Said he had to come clean, that he never meant to hurt me, that it just happened, yadda yadda. He has a solid alibi for the time of death, though. He was on a fishing trip in the Uintas with his son's Scouts troop. He didn't kill her. I'm sure of it."

Taylor wasn't nearly as convinced. If John Randall was cold-blooded enough to carry on an affair with Dru right under Hunter's nose, he might just be capable of anything. She suddenly wanted to talk to Wyatt about this, to get his perspective.

"Was your house completely destroyed?" Hunter asked, distracting her from her thoughts.

She shifted gears. "Yes. Nothing left but some timbers."

"I'm sorry. I know how much you loved that little place. I guess Kate wasn't hurt or Martin would have told me."

What was that odd note in his voice? she wondered, then

just assumed it was the unreliable cellular connection. "She wasn't even in the country. She went to Central America again with that medical team she worked with."

"Good."

"We're both doing okay," she said. "We're slowly starting to replace our stuff."

"Where are you staying?" he asked.

"Eventually we'll probably find another place in town but for now we're staying at your place in the canyon. I hope that's okay."

"Of course. It belongs to you as much as it does me."

"It's been good to air out the house for a while. Belle's having a great time chasing squirrels."

He actually laughed at that—a rare enough sound that it stopped her in her tracks.

"That dog never met a squirrel she didn't like. Toss a few sticks to her for me, would you?"

She had to swallow a couple of times before she trusted her voice. "I will," she promised.

When he spoke again, any levity had been erased from his voice as if it never existed. "And promise me you'll let Martin and his private investigators handle the appeal. It's hell enough in here, Tay. If something happened to you out there because of my case, I wouldn't be able to bear it."

"I'll be fine," she said.

"You know, I can always call Martin and tell him I want to drop any efforts to appeal. If you keep putting yourself in danger, that's exactly what I'll do. It's not worth your life."

She heard the emotion in his voice, emotion he rarely showed, and this time even swallowing hard wasn't enough to keep down her tears. She closed her eyes. No matter how upset it made him, she knew she couldn't promise him that.

"I'm fine," she repeated. "Just take care of yourself."

She hung up before he could argue, then sank down on a bench outside the law library, fighting with everything inside her to give in to the urge to bury her head in her arms and weep for her brother and all he had been forced to endure.

She wouldn't give in, though. She wouldn't give in and she wouldn't give up. They were close, she knew it.

Because her feelings were so tender and raw, she had avoided talking with Wyatt for four days, since that terrible lunch when he hadn't been able to take his eyes off Kate. He had called her several times, but when she recognized the caller ID she had let his call go to voice mail.

If she hadn't been acting like a stupid, hurt little girl, who knew how much progress she and Wyatt could have made in those four days toward figuring out who really killed Dru and Mickie?

She needed to get over it—or at least hide her feelings deep inside her so they could resume their working relationship, if nothing else.

She would call him, she decided. She could use the new information about John Randall as a reason and try to set up another meeting with him. Her heart pounding, she dialed his cell phone. This time she was the one sent to voice mail.

How pathetic was she that her stomach fluttered just hearing his recorded message, saying in that sexy deep voice that he was not currently available?

She left him a quick message to call her, then sat in the cool sunshine for a few moments more, trying to process all the information they had collected so far.

If the father of Dru's baby wasn't the killer—and she still wasn't willing to discount that, despite Hunter's assertion that John Randall was out of town—who was left?

She ticked off the possibilities in her mind. Dru had been about to break open a police corruption story, so any of the primary targets of that exposé would have had reason to want her dead. They needed to press Mike Thurman for names—see what they could squeeze out.

And what about Mickie? She hadn't forgotten her thought the other day that perhaps Mickie had been the target all along. It was worthy of further scrutiny—and the only thing she had to go on right now was Mickie's obsession with an old case.

That was as good a place as any to start, she decided. And what better place to look up information on an old case than the law library? She decided the world wouldn't stop turning if she blew off her class.

Behind the reference desk, Barbara smiled when she saw Taylor. "Can't you get enough of this place?"

"Guess not," Taylor answered. "I was remembering the other day when you mentioned that old case Mickie was so interested in. I'd like to look at anything you might have on it."

Barbara made a wry face. "You could if it was available, but I'm afraid another patron beat you to it."

What were the odds that someone else would be interested in the exact same thirty-year-old case? She frowned and was about to ask, when Barbara gestured to the table behind her.

Everything made sense when she saw Wyatt with books and papers spread out around him. He was wearing those sexy reading glasses he used sometimes and looked so gorgeous she couldn't breathe.

Despite the message she'd left for him, she wasn't sure she was ready to talk to him yet. She needed more time to ready her defenses. She thought about slipping back through the glass doors but he looked up from his books, just then and caught her gaze.

The delight on his face took her by surprise. Maybe he thought Kate was with her, she thought sourly. No, that wasn't fair. He had been nothing but kind to her. It wasn't his fault that she wanted more.

"I'm afraid Wyatt beat you to the citation by about a half hour," Barbara said.

Taylor let out the breath she hadn't realized she had been holding. "Maybe I can talk him into sharing," she murmured, then forced herself to walk briskly toward his table before she lost her nerve.

Chapter 12

"I wondered if I might bump into you today," Wyatt said, trying his level best to tamp down the joy bursting through him like a lit box of Roman candles.

Only when he saw her standing there by the reference desk did he admit to himself that he had been spending half the afternoon watching for her, anticipating just this kind of encounter.

He shouldn't be this ecstatic to see her, shouldn't want to pull her close and kiss that perpetual worry from her forehead.

He had missed her these past few days. He hadn't realized exactly how much—how dry and empty his life suddenly seemed without her—until right this moment, when this sweet sense of rightness filled him.

He had almost called her a dozen times in the past few days. The night before, he had even driven up Little Cottonwood Canyon to talk to her, but had turned around before he reached her family's cabin.

Not yet. He didn't want to run the risk of Kate Spencer answering the door or picking up the phone. When he saw her again, Wyatt wasn't sure he would be able to hold back the avalanche of questions waiting to break free.

Until he could obtain the results of the DNA tests he and Gage had arranged, he thought it would be better if he avoided Kate altogether, which he had discovered had the unfortunate side effect of also forcing him to avoid Taylor.

It didn't keep her from consuming his thoughts, though. Partly to distract him from the two women he suddenly couldn't stop thinking about—though for entirely different reasons—he had spent the weekend at hard physical labor, working with his foreman to ready the ranch for the heavy winter snows he knew were on the horizon. The work had the desired effect of tiring his body enough that he could sleep. If not for that, he knew he would have burned all night for Taylor.

As it was, he woke up hard and hungry from dreaming of her.

Right now, she wore khaki pants, a crisp white shirt and a soft sweater the color of the sagebrush that dotted the foothills—and his mouth watered just looking at her.

He wondered what all these eager young law students working so feverishly at carrels all around them would do if he slipped off that soft sweater, worked a few buttons of her blouse free and started nibbling on the delectable hollows at her throat.

With an internal groan, he forced himself to get control of his unruly desire. No sense torturing himself when he couldn't do anything about it—especially when he *wouldn't* do anything, even if he could.

"Hello," she murmured, and to his surprise, her voice was

as cool and remote as the Klondike and her eyes were just as chilly.

He racked his brain to think what might have set her off but couldn't think of anything.

"How have you been?" he finally asked. "Have you found another place to live yet?"

She shook her head. "We're still staying at the cabin. As soon as the snow flies I'm sure Kate and I will both want something a little closer to town, but for now it's working out."

"Good. I've been worrying about you."

"Well, cut it out." She shoved her bag onto the table with jerky movements. "I don't need you or anyone else worrying about me."

Something was up. Everything about her screamed tension, from her stiff shoulders to the tightly pursed mouth and those cool, remote eyes. "What's wrong?"

She paused as if she didn't want to answer him—or if she had so many things wrong she didn't know where to start—then she shrugged. "I just had an angry call from my dear brother who found out about the house fire. Now he wants me to hide away somewhere and give up. If I don't stop trying to find out who really killed Dru and Mickie, he threatened to drop any efforts to appeal. He's just going to let them kill him because he thinks I can't take care of myself."

"Are you going to stop?"

The tension in her lovely, fine-boned features turned to resolution. "What do you think?"

"I think you're a stubborn woman, Taylor Bradshaw."

"Not stubborn. Determined. I'm close. I can feel it, Wyatt. So can you. We're heading in the right direction. It's just a matter of figuring out what route will get us there."

She sat in the chair next to him and he cursed himself for reacting to the sweet smell of wildflowers.

"I did learn something during my conversation with Hunter. He knows who fathered Dru's baby. Get this—Dru was having an affair with Hunter's partner, John Randall."

"No kidding?" How did this new information fit into this most puzzling of cases? Wyatt wondered.

"Hunter claims he has an alibi and was hiking in the backcountry at the time of the murder, but I want to talk to Martin about having his private investigator look into it. See how good his alibi really is."

"And if you find out it was airtight?"

"Then I'll try another road. What else can I do?" She scanned the books he had been studying. "Barbara says you're looking at the appeal in the Valencia case. Anything interesting?"

He shrugged. "It's an interesting case. I went to the courthouse last week and made a copy of the court transcript of the original trial, and finally read through it last night. This morning I looked up press coverage from the time, and now I'm looking for the appeal briefs—but so far I'm coming up empty as to what might have interested Mickie about it. It seems like a pretty cut-and-dried case. I can't find anything out of the ordinary."

"What can you tell me about it?" Taylor slipped off her sweater and hung it on the back of her chair, then sat so she could get down to business.

Wyatt was fascinated by the way she seemed to neatly store away her emotions and concentrate on the matter at hand.

"It's a murder trial," he answered. "A fairly grisly one involving the kidnapping, rape and murder of an eight-year-old girl."

She made an instinctive exclamation of revulsion.

"Yeah. Not exactly the kind of pleasant reading you might expect for someone in her last days of life."

"What are the details?" she asked.

He scanned the neatly organized documents in front of him. "In 1974, a handyman by the name of Paul Valencia was arrested and charged with capital homicide after a massive manhunt. From the newspaper accounts, I gather there was a huge public outcry to find the person responsible. Valencia had already done a stint in prison for robbery and his finger-prints were linked to evidence at the murder scene. Other than that, the case against him seems largely circumstantial."

"But he was convicted, obviously."

Wyatt nodded. "It all seems fairly routine, as far as I can tell. One interesting note—there are some familiar names in-volved in the case. Big ones. Your father was on the bench."

He was interested to see her reaction to that bit of infor-mation, but his mention of her father only earned him an im-passive look.

"Anyone else I would recognize?" she asked.

"Denny Sullivan and Kyle Dougherty."

Though she hadn't responded to learning her father had been involved in the case, her eyes widened at the names of the current police chief and the state attorney general. "A couple of big guns."

"Sullivan was the lead detective and the one who arrested Valencia, and Dougherty was the prosecuting attorney. I get the feeling this was a watershed case for everybody involved. One of those career-makers."

Though the court proceedings looked routine, Wyatt had to admit he found the case fascinating. This was the part of his job he loved, digging into the past and fleshing out the bare bones of cases. Maybe he could file this one away for a future project—except that he didn't like writing about cases with child victims.

That was one area where he and Gage differed. Wyatt avoided writing about cases involving kids. He didn't know if he had the mental fortitude necessary to dig so deeply into the psyche of someone who would hurt a child. Gage, on the other hand, had spent much of his career in the FBI's Crimes Against Children unit.

Wyatt pushed away the reflection and focused on Taylor once more. "You'll also be interested to know our friend Martin James was the man's defense attorney."

"Thirty years ago." She processed the information. "That must have been early in his career too."

"Right. I don't think there was much he could have done to help Valencia, though. The jury took less than an hour to come back with a guilty verdict. His appeal was denied and Valencia was executed by firing squad three years later."

She visibly shuddered, her fingers tightening on the edge of the table, and he knew she must be thinking of Hunter.

"Did you find any connection to Mickie in anything you've read?" she asked after a moment.

"No. Her name isn't mentioned anywhere in the briefs. But she worked in the prosecutor's office so maybe she assisted the state's case. Or maybe she was just interested in it."

"Why?"

"We may never know the answer to that."

They lapsed into silence, both trying to figure out where they should go from here.

Wyatt wasn't very good for her concentration, Taylor decided. She was intensely aware of him and hated it. They sat close enough that his subtle aftershave drifted to her, an erotic combination of leather and sage, and despite the seriousness of their task, she had a hard time focusing on anything but the memory of their heated kiss the other night at his soothing creek-side retreat.

She did her best to push the memory away. "Maybe I need to ask Martin if he remembers the case," she said. "I hounded his secretary into carving out a quick appointment for me to talk about the briefs he's readying for Hunter's appeal. He was in court all day today, so tomorrow is the earliest I can meet with him. I'll bring this up too."

"I'll come with you."

She shook her head. "I wouldn't ask you to drive down to the city from Liberty two days in a row."

"I'm staying at my apartment for a while. I've got a couple of projects in the works and thought it would be better to stay close to town in case something breaks."

He avoided her gaze when he spoke, and she couldn't help wondering at his evasiveness. What was he keeping from her? Probably nothing at all to do with Hunter's case, she chastised herself. The man had a life away from her and her troubles. She shouldn't be narcissistic enough to think his world revolved around her.

"Look, I think I'm done here. I know it's early but why don't we go grab a bite to eat and we can talk strategy before you meet with Martin?" Wyatt suggested. "I didn't take time for lunch and I'm starving."

She wasn't sure she wanted to share a meal with him again, not after their last disaster. Of course, Kate was working a double shift at the hospital and wouldn't be anywhere around. Still, she knew spending more time with him wasn't the greatest idea.

"You have to eat," Wyatt pressed. "Come on, I'll treat you to a sandwich."

She was so weak when it came to Wyatt McKinnon, Taylor thought as she heard herself agreeing. "Let me put my books in my carrel so I don't have to lug them with me."

"I made copies of everything I need on the Valencia case. Do you want to take what I have and read through it? You're the law student, so maybe you can see something in there I missed."

"Sure," she said, trying to figure out how she could fit in any more reading.

Wyatt followed her to the second floor of the library where her carrel was tucked away on the inside wall behind the tax alcove. She unlocked her cabinet and shoved her bag in, then noticed a paper facedown on the desk. Sometimes the library staff or law faculty left notes to students about routine maintenance or special events. Assuming it was something like that, she turned it over.

She frowned in confusion. Why would someone send her a story from a Nevada newspaper?

She read the headline and her blood turned to ice.

The story was about a death-row inmate in Nevada who killed another inmate with a homemade shiv in what authorities believed was a hit ordered from outside the prison walls.

In a typewritten note at the bottom of the photocopied article was a message for her:

EASY ENOUGH TO ARRANGE WHEN YOU HAVE NOTHING TO LOSE.

Wyatt wasn't sure what was happening. One moment, she was storing her gear inside the glass-fronted cabinet above her study desk, the next she sank bonelessly into her chair.

"Taylor? Everything okay?" he asked.

She gazed at him blankly, as if she'd forgotten he was even there, then without a word she handed him the paper. He scanned it quickly, registering the ominous note.

The implication was clear—she could forget about waiting for state-sponsored capital punishment. If she didn't back off, her brother would die violently in prison before the high court even had a chance to look at any appeal.

Guilty or not, Hunter Bradshaw would pay the ultimate price inside prison.

What kind of bastard would use her love for her brother as a billy club against her? He growled a long, colorful string of oaths but reined in his temper when he saw her skin was as pale as the paper he held in his hands and her eyes had a hollow, shocky look to them.

She couldn't take much more of this, he realized. In the past few weeks she had sustained stress after stress and he could see it was beginning to take its toll on her. The urge to protect her, to tuck her against him and keep her safe, just about overwhelmed him.

His first step was dragging her out of there.

"You need some air. Come on," he ordered.

He took a moment to slip the note into a page protector from his bag to preserve any fingerprints that might be there—though he doubted they would be that lucky—then grabbed her elbow and walked with her out into the cool beauty of a fall afternoon.

The sky was vividly blue with only a few plump clouds floating across its wide expanse, but Wyatt barely noticed, consumed only with taking care of her, with seeing some color return to her face and that numb look leave her blue eyes.

"I have to warn him," Taylor said when they were outside. "I have to let him know he's in danger."

"We can phone the corrections department and make sure

they're up to speed on what's been going on," he answered. "They'll take protective measures."

"It won't be enough. I'm not naive, Wyatt. I know how dangerous life can be on the inside. Like the note says, his murder would be easy enough to arrange. He's in there with violent men who have already committed terrible crimes. What's one more? Most of them already hate him because he was a cop and would be only too willing to do this. What repercussions would there be? There's only so much you can do to punish a man who's already on death row."

To his frustration, he didn't have any answers. The hell of it was, she was right. Hunter Bradshaw could be stabbed with a shiv in the gut tomorrow and most people in the state would think whoever killed him had simply saved the state the trouble.

They walked in silence for a few more moments until they reached a quiet corner of campus, with several benches and a burbling fountain. Taylor took one of the nearby benches and Wyatt sat beside her, feeling about as powerless as he ever had.

More than anything, he wished he had the words to ease her fear for her brother, but he knew there was nothing he could say.

"Our mother died when I was six. Hunter was twelve." Taylor stared at the fountain as she spoke, lost in a past he couldn't see. "She stuck one of the Judge's antique revolvers in her mouth and pulled the trigger. Hunter found her."

His insides tightened at her cool, emotionless voice, at the grim picture she painted. He would have thought her made of ice except her knuckles were white where her fists gripped her knees. "Oh, Taylor. I didn't know. I'm so sorry."

"Even when she was alive she was…ill. She had wild, violent mood swings. She seemed to tolerate Hunter, but for some reason something about me seemed to set her off. She would be loving and kind one second and then lash out furiously the next. She could be brushing my hair, talking about how pretty it was, like cinnamon in the sunlight, then she would suddenly try to yank it out from the roots. It was a…difficult childhood."

The understatement just about sent him to his knees. How had she survived? he wondered. How could any child?

She answered his unspoken question. "Hunter was always there. He protected me, cared for me. Loved me. After our mother died, the Judge hired a series of housekeepers but they were employees. They did their job but without much in the way of love and affection. Our father was a very busy, very important man. But Hunter was never too busy for me. Even when he was a teenager and constantly at odds with our father, he always made time for his bratty little sister."

He was stunned that she would tell him this—the depth of her trust in him staggered him. In all the research he had done about her family, about Hunter's childhood, he had never unearthed this information or any whisper that Angela Bradshaw had suffered from mental illness and killed herself. The judge must have covered it up to keep it from the media. With his connections, that didn't surprise him. He probably never would have known if Taylor hadn't confided in him.

Her words definitely gave him new insight into the complicated man he had met in prison, Wyatt thought. The man had found his mother's body, had protected his little sister from the woman's wild mood swings. It would make a hell of a hook, but he knew he could never use this information. She had taken a huge leap of faith to confide in him and he refused to let her suffer for that by revealing her dark family secrets to the world.

"He always looked out for me," she continued. "Now it's my turn to look out for him—and I'm failing."

Tears pooled in those blue eyes and a single drop trickled out of the corner of one and trailed down her cheek. Wyatt groaned and reached for her, pulling her into his arms.

"You're not. You're doing everything possible to free him."

"It's not enough. You have no idea how helpless I feel, knowing there's nothing I can do to help him."

"If anybody understands, Tay, I do," he answered, his voice rough.

For a moment, she looked at him blankly, and then he saw understanding flicker in her eyes—they darkened with empathy. She touched his cheek with a tenderness that took his breath away.

"I'm sorry," she murmured. "You're right. I'm afraid I've become very self-absorbed these past few months. I forget about your sister—and that others carry their own burdens."

The urge to tell her about Kate and his suspicions was so powerful that the words swelled in his throat and hovered there, but he somehow managed to swallow them down.

He couldn't tell her , at least until he had something more substantial to share.

He settled for softly pressing his mouth to those fingers she still held against his cheek.

Her hands trembled and a delicate shiver rippled across her shoulders. Sunshine shot golden threads through her hair and she closed her eyes and leaned into him.

And Wyatt knew he was lost.

Chapter 13

His kiss was slow, tender, sweet, and her heart seemed to give a long sigh of welcome.

Her arms curled up against his chest and she breathed in that clean male scent of him, wanting to burn it into her brain cells. For a few moments she let herself forget about the newspaper article left on her carrel, forget his odd reaction to Kate the other day, forget everything but this aching tenderness.

In his arms, her burdens didn't feel nearly so heavy, and for the first time in days she let herself fully relax.

Before their kiss, she had been so tired, she thought as she leaned against him. Tired of the constant worry and of the finely wrought tension between her and Wyatt.

But in his arms, her fatigue seemed to bubble away like the water flowing over the fountain's lip, leaving an odd contentment in its wake.

He pulled her closer until she was almost on his lap, and she wanted to be nowhere else on earth.

After several long, intoxicating moments, he drew in a ragged breath and stilled the soft caress of his fingers. "We've got to stop doing this," he murmured, regret in his voice.

Her thoughts were a soft, dreamy haze and she could only manage to form one semi-coherent word. "Why?"

His laugh sounded rough, ragged. "Now there's a good question, Counselor. For one thing, we're in a public place. Much more of this and I don't think I'll be able to prevent making a spectacle of both of us to any unsuspecting passersby."

She blinked back to awareness and realized her shirt was untucked and they were both breathing hard. Although they were in a semi-secluded spot, shielded from view on nearly every side by trees and bushes, from the right angle, anyone might be able to see them.

Heat singed her cheeks. How could she have forgotten herself so completely? For a woman who valued control, knowing she could lose it so easily with Wyatt—could forget where she was, what she should be doing—was a terrifying, mortifying concept.

She didn't understand this man. How could he have looked so completely gobsmacked when he saw Kate and still gaze at Taylor with such tenderness in those green eyes?

"You're killing me, Taylor." His voice was so low she had to strain to hear above the fountain. "You have to know that. If circumstances were different, you and I would both be naked on this bench right now."

She shivered at the intensity in his voice and the image his words conjured up. Her breasts ached and her insides did a long slow roll. She wanted that so much—wanted *him*—that she couldn't seem to breathe around it. Okay, not here on a campus bench, maybe, but if they were somewhere else, she wasn't sure she would be able to stop.

To cover her reaction, she forced herself to joke. "Wouldn't the papers just go to town with that one? Utah's sexiest best-selling author caught in campus romp with sister of notorious felon."

His short laugh sounded strained. He looked as if he wanted to say more, but the moment passed.

"Thank you for the listening ear and for…everything else. Believe it or not, I feel better."

"Glad one of us does," he muttered.

She surprised both of them by laughing at his disgruntled tone. When he stared at her, an odd light in his eyes, she realized how seldom she must laugh anymore. She hadn't found many things amusing since Hunter's arrest.

No matter how things turned out, she needed to change that, she decided. Her brother was right, she couldn't put her life on hold forever.

"I'd better go. I'm afraid I won't have time to eat with you after all. My study group will be waiting."

Disappointment marked his frown, but he nodded. "I'll walk you back to the library. Just give me a minute."

Taylor was intensely conscious of him as they sat in the fading autumn sunlight while the cool fall air caressed them and the fountain gurgled in the background.

After a moment, he stood up. "I think I'm ready."

Her awareness of him didn't ease as they walked back to the library. She caught herself appreciating his lean, rangy build and his confident stride.

"What about the letter?" he asked when they neared the law complex. "Will you go the police?"

"With what? A photocopied newspaper article? They'll laugh me right out of the station."

"You were probably too shell-shocked to notice, but I put the note in a page protector, just in case any fingerprints could be lifted. Do you mind if I give it to Gage to run through the FBI lab?"

"I thought he and Allie were still on their honeymoon."

"They returned over the weekend. I'm sure he would do what he could to help us."

Us. What strength was contained in that tiny word! She found it soothing and comforting and empowering, even if it was only an illusion. She and Wyatt were not an *us.* They weren't an anything.

"You can certainly give it to him," she answered. "But I doubt he'll find anything useful."

"You're probably right, but it's worth a shot." He paused. "Who knew that was your *particular* carrel?"

She had been wondering the same thing. "Other second-years. My professors. Dozens of people. It would be easy for anyone to find out, really, simply by asking the right person."

"I'm sure the library has an extensive security camera system that most likely captured whoever left it there. But unless we get the police involved, we won't be able to access those tapes."

"The police aren't going to be interested, Wyatt. You and I both know that. It wasn't even a threat really, just a small comment about a newspaper article."

"You know better than that. We both do," he said. "The bastard knew just what he was doing—threatening you didn't work, so he found something even better. Threatening your brother."

As tactics go, it was vicious and low and remarkably effective. She knew she would have a difficult time focusing on the case. She lived daily with the knowledge that her brother faced death, but now that menace was far more immediate, far more *real*.

Even with that shadow hanging over her, she couldn't quit. "I told you I'm meeting with Martin tomorrow for an update," she said. "I'll let you know how things go."

"I should be at the apartment all day. I gave you the address and phone number, and you have my cell. I've got weeks' worth of correspondence to catch up on and promised myself I wouldn't move from my computer until I was finished."

"I'll call you after my appointment."

"Be careful, Tay. Promise me that."

She had to admit his concern warmed her, she thought as she nodded agreement, and made the world seem just a little less dark and scary.

In his elegantly appointed offices in the historic Judge Building the next morning, Martin greeted her with his usual hug and kiss on the cheek, but she could already see distracted shadows in his eyes.

"I've got about ten minutes before I have to leave for a meeting with the prosecutor's office about a plea deal for another client, so we'll have to do this fast."

Taylor took the comfortable leather wingback he gestured her to, trying to tamp down the familiar frustration churning through her. Every time she met Martin the conversation seemed to run along the same channels. He was always distracted and evasive, she was always pushy and impatient.

"Thank you for making time to meet with me," she said. "How is Judy?"

"Good. She's spoiling herself at Green Valley Spa in St. George for the week. It was my anniversary present to her."

Judy James was one of the kindest, most gracious women Taylor knew. At one time or another, Martin's wife had served on just about every charitable committee in town, and she loved entertaining and supporting arts and culture in the valley.

"What can I do for you, Taylor?"

Martin's brusqueness took her by surprise, jarring her from fond thoughts of his wife. Instead of sitting beside her on the other armchair, he had taken a place behind his desk. In any other man, she would have seen it as a power play, but this was Martin.

"I'm sure you can guess. I wanted an update on the appeal."

"It's going well," he said. "I expect to be filing several briefs in the coming weeks."

"That's what you've been saying for the past three months." She leaned forward, trying not to sound encroaching or managing. "If it will help, I've found some new information that might be relevant to your briefs."

His hand tightened on the expensive pen he was using to jot a note in his planner. He gazed at her with paternal concern. "You're becoming obsessed, Taylor. I've said this before but I mean it this time. You need to develop some outside interests beyond your brother's case. You've dropped out of med school, given up your life's dream, sacrificed everything for Hunter. Your father wouldn't be happy about this."

"The Judge wanted both Hunter and me to follow in his grand judicial footsteps. You know he refused to pay one cent toward medical school and was livid with Hunter for becoming a cop. He would be ecstatic that one of us ended up in law school—maybe not the circumstances that led me to it, but the end result."

"You're right about that. I know it was his fondest dream that one of you pass the bar, but he wouldn't have wanted it this way."

"We deal with what we're given, Martin. You're the one who taught me that."

He didn't answer, and she took that as encouragement to outline for him the various theories she and Wyatt had developed. Knowing her time was limited, she spoke quickly and concisely.

Martin took a few notes here and there but didn't seem overly enthusiastic about any of their new information. At least he was listening, though. She had to give him points for that.

"One more odd thing I wanted to ask you about—" She spoke quickly, knowing her ten minutes had been up at least five minutes ago. "Do you remember the Paul Valencia case?"

The pen slipped from his fingers and would have rolled from the desk to the floor but he quickly caught it. "Of course I do. How could I forget? It's one of only two death penalty cases I've ever lost."

Hunter was the other one, she realized. Was there something significant in that fact?

"I know it was a long time ago, but do you remember if Mickie Wallace Ferrin was involved in the trial proceedings at all? She worked for the prosecutor's office at the time."

He looked annoyed at the question. "I don't know. She could have been. It was a long time ago. Anyway, what does any of that have to do with Hunter?"

"I don't know. Probably nothing. But she apparently spent some time researching the case right before her death. I just found it odd that she could barely get out of bed from the effects of radiation and chemo but she dragged herself to Quinney to look through *Pacific Reporters*. Don't you find that strange?"

"People who are dying do odd things. I think you're desperate and are willing to follow any wild guess."

She gazed at him, startled by his bluntness. When he rose and started stuffing files into his briefcase as if their interview was over, her dander rose right along with him.

"I still think it's worth investigating. I've written up everything I've found to date about the Valencia case and about the other possible angles—Dru's investigation into police corruption and the threats she received before her death. Surely we can raise enough question of reasonable doubt to have his case re-examined."

He paused, his hands still in his briefcase. The look he gave her stunned her with its bitterness.

"*You* might have all the time in the world to rush off on any goose chase that comes along, but I've got other clients here."

She rose as well. "I know you're busy, Martin, but this is important! This is Hunter's life we're talking about here."

"You can cut the melodrama, Taylor. I know it's Hunter's life. It's a little hard for me to forget that, when you keep throwing it in my face every chance you get."

She curled her hands into fists and, after months of placating and appeasing, finally lost her temper. "If you won't help me prove he's innocent, maybe I need to find somebody else who will. Somebody who might at least pretend to give half a damn that the state is willing to execute an innocent man. Somebody more concerned about justice than about his billable hours."

Martin's face turned an alarming shade of red, and she saw a vein work in his neck.

"You're too wrapped up in your illusions to face reality," he snapped. "Your brother is guilty as hell. Why can't you get that through your head?"

She stared at him. "You don't believe that."

"He killed those women in a jealous rage. I know it, the

jury knew it, the whole damn state knows it. You're the only one who's either too stupid or too loyal to figure out he deserves a needle in the arm."

Taylor swayed from both the unexpectedness and the brutality of the attack and had to grab the edge of the desk between them to keep from falling into her chair. Her head felt light, woolly, while bike churned in her throat.

How could this be Martin saying these terrible things? The avuncular family friend, Hunter's own attorney? He was supposed to be her brother's most valiant, loyal defender! For him to go on the attack like this seemed a betrayal of the worst sort.

She straightened her spine, drawing on whatever low reserves of strength she had left. "I guess I don't need to tell you you're fired," she said, her voice low. Then, with mechanical movements, she gathered her things and walked out of his office.

She made it to her car before the trembling started. She wasn't sure if it stemmed from anger, shock or dismay—or a combination of all three.

At last she understood why Martin had been dragging his feet all these months on the appeal. Why he dodged her calls and ignored her e-mails—because he didn't *want* to prove Hunter's innocence.

How could Martin believe such terrible things? He *knew* Hunter, had since Hunter was a child. He had to see what he was—and wasn't—capable of.

All this time when he had pretended he was right there in the trenches with her, fighting just as hard as she was for Hunter's life, he hadn't believed the things he was saying. How much had his opinion about Hunter's guilt filtered through to his performance in the courtroom during the trial? she wondered.

Her stomach was tangled up in knots of betrayal and hurt

and as she sat in her car while a cold November rain pelted her windshield, she felt truly alone.

No. Not completely, she reminded herself. She still had Wyatt, who had provided her unwavering support these past weeks.

Even if he still said he was withholding judgment about Hunter's guilt or innocence, at least he was keeping the possibility open—unlike Martin, who had apparently made up his mind before the trial ever started.

The need to see him, to soak up that support like the ground welcomed the rain, consumed her. With a quick twist of her wrist, she started her car and pulled out of the parking lot, then turned north toward his condominium.

When she was twelve years old, Dru Ferrin tossed her long wheat-colored hair behind her shoulders and announced to the rest of her seventh grade English class at Huntsville Middle School that one day everyone in Utah would know her name. She would be famous, she promised. Just wait and see.

Dru couldn't have known during those boastful school days just how right her prediction would prove— or the vicious crime that would…

The doorbell suddenly rang through his comfortable two-bedroom apartment and Wyatt growled a curse.

He thought about ignoring it so he could try to at least finish writing the first page, but the doorbell rang again, this time more insistently, and Wyatt gave up trying to chase after the runaway train of thought.

He hated interruptions while he was working, he thought as he saved the few paltry words and put his laptop to sleep.

He could write under a wide variety of conditions—in the mountains, in his truck, even on horseback with a pen and paper—but when he was in the groove, he preferred peace and quiet and a minimum of disturbances.

He was scowling when he thrust open the door, but his irritation disappeared when he found Taylor standing on the other side. He had time only to register her wan features and wounded eyes before she launched into his arms.

He wasn't one to turn away a warm, sexy woman when she jumped him, but he knew this wasn't normal behavior for Taylor. Baffled concern washed through him even as he fought awareness of her soft, feminine curves.

"What's wrong?" he asked.

"Nothing," she mumbled, burrowing even closer.

How was it that a tall, willowy woman like Taylor could at times feel so small and fragile? he wondered.

"I just needed to see you," she said in a low voice.

Under other circumstances he might have been flattered, but he knew something was up. It didn't take a huge leap in logic to make the connection, not when he remembered what had been on her agenda that day. "You were meeting Martin this morning. Did something happen?"

She was quiet for several moments and then, to his regret, she slid out of his arms and gathered composure around her like a sari.

"You could say that. He told me I was wasting my time fighting Hunter's execution. I believe his exact words were that Hunter is 'guilty as hell' and something to the effect that I'm the only one too stupid to figure out Hunter deserves a needle in his arm."

White-hot rage filled him. Dammit. Now he knew why he had never liked the bastard. Martin was supposed to be a friend, an ally—how could he turn on her like that?

He pulled her back into his arms, wishing there was more he could do to comfort her. "I'm sorry."

"I fired him, of course."

"Good."

She sighed. "Though I suppose technically I don't have the right to do that, only Hunter does. But since the Bradshaw family trust is footing the bill and I'm the sole executor with Hunter in prison, I guess that gives me some say. So now I need to find another defense attorney and bring him up to speed on the appeal."

"I know some good ones. I can help hook you up."

"Thank you."

She was quiet for several moments, although her body still trembled slightly in his arms. "I lost so many friends after Hunter was arrested, so many people who should have stood behind Hunter and didn't. I was nearly engaged at the time of the murders, did you know that?"

He had no right to be jealous, Wyatt told himself.

"But Rob didn't want the taint of marrying a woman whose brother was a convicted murderer," she said. "He broke things off the day Hunter was charged. Others were the same way, but not Martin and Judy. I thought they had the same faith in his innocence that I did."

"I'm sorry," he said again.

"I know," she murmured, then lifted her gaze to his. "You know, after all those terrible things Martin said, I only had one thought in my mind."

The emotion pooled in those lovely blue depths stunned him, left him feeling breathless. "What?"

"Finding you. I knew you would help me not to hurt so much."

Before he could process her stunning words—or figure out why they seemed to peel back every protective layer he had encasing his heart—she wrapped her arms around his neck and pulled his mouth down to hers.

He froze for a moment as shock and need and tenderness exploded inside him, and then, with a low, strangled sound, he kissed her back.

Chapter 14

Taylor sighed and settled into his arms as if she had been waiting her entire life for just this moment.

She smelled of wildflowers and tasted of coffee and mint. He found the combination incredibly arousing—but then, he found everything about her arousing, from the tiny gold hoops in her ears to the tantalizing glimpse of creamy collarbone through her crisp white shirt to those unbelievably long legs.

Every time they kissed had been intense—an odd mix of tenderness and heat. But something was different this time, he sensed. He couldn't put a finger on exactly what, but everything seemed richer, more vibrant.

Before, she always seemed to hold something back—or maybe it was him, he admitted—but now she kissed him with an eagerness that sent blood instantly surging to his groin.

She sighed his name and the sound was so powerful that his brain seemed to freeze. He forgot all his reasons not to complicate things between them and gave in to the raging need inside him.

Somehow—he wasn't sure just how—they made it to the couch. With a low sound of arousal in her throat, she pulled him down until their bodies connected at a hundred pulse points. Ah. Bliss. This was what he craved, what he had been craving for weeks.

No, months, he acknowledged. He had wanted her since those first days in the trial. His desire had been all tangled up, first with those early protective instincts and now with this terrifying tenderness.

Despite all his efforts to keep his distance, he was crazy about her, he admitted to himself. Objectivity, hell. He hadn't been objective about Taylor Bradshaw since the day he met her.

He sighed and deepened the kiss. On a sexy, breathy little moan, she parted her lips and he slipped inside her mouth, exploring and tasting and savoring.

He was vaguely conscious of her hands tugging his shirt free of his jeans, of those long, cool fingers slipping inside his shirt to splay across the skin of his back, but he was too busy with his own explorations to do more than shudder in response.

"Did I hurt you?" she asked, concern in her voice.

"Mmm" was the only sound he could manage to make as he left her mouth to trail kisses down that long, elegant column of throat to the hollow just below her collarbone.

Her skin was warm and soft, delicious. She arched to meet his mouth and, through the open neck of her shirt, he saw her pulse beat just above her sternum like a frantic little chick.

He kissed that fluttering pulse and was rewarded with a breathy sigh, all the encouragement he needed to explore farther, to slip a button free and press his mouth to the slope of one high, firm breast.

This time her sigh was definitely a moan. With hands he was embarrassed to see trembling, he worked another button free, revealing an erotic glimpse of a lacy peach bra that made him think of hot summer nights and juice dripping off his chin.

She leaned against his hand and he took that as permission to unbutton the shirt completely. His mouth went dry at the erotic sight of her in those sexy tailored slacks and a peach bra, nothing else.

"You've been shopping," he murmured.

"What?" she asked blankly.

He slid a finger under a silky peach strap and tugged a little. "I don't remember this from our little trip to the mall. If I had, believe me, I doubt I would have been able to sleep for the past two weeks, imagining you in it just like this. Long and sleek and gorgeous."

"You were there." Her voice sounded breathless, aroused. "I picked it out while you were busy watching the basketball game on a dozen screens in the electronics department."

"I missed out on *this* to watch a stupid basketball game?"

She laughed, and he decided he would never get tired of that sound. He vowed he would try to do everything he could to make sure she had plenty of practice.

"You're seeing it now," she murmured. "That counts for something, doesn't it?"

The heat in his gaze was all the answer she needed. This was right, she thought. She loved this man with all her heart and she fiercely wanted to be with him. She might have to endure heartache later, but for now she vowed to sit back and enjoy the ride.

"The bra is part of a matched set," she added with a sidelong look. "Just in case you might be interested in seeing the rest."

He groaned and closed his eyes. When he opened them, they were hot and hungry and her insides trembled in reaction.

Before she could speak, he scooped her up in one smooth motion and carried her into the bedroom. He might look lean, but there were definitely muscles there, she thought as anticipation curled through her like ribbons on a birthday present.

After lowering her to the bed, he reached for the button on her trousers, but her hands stopped him. "No fair. You're still dressed."

"I only have on boring blue boxers, not delectable, delicious, de-lovely peach fantasies."

"That's a great comfort," she murmured. "I believe I prefer the idea of you wearing boxers rather than lacy peach thingies."

He laughed and kissed her forehead, but complied with her wishes and unbuttoned his jeans, then quickly slipped out of them before reaching for her.

That little shopping side trip had been worth every moment, she thought later after, she had slipped out of everything but her lingerie. Wyatt gazed down at her with that hot, hungry look blazing in his eyes.

"I don't think I'll ever be able to taste a peach again without thinking of this moment," he said, then leaned down to kiss her mouth softly.

The poignancy of his kiss brought tears to her eyes but she blinked them away. No regrets. She wanted to savor this moment forever, not ruin it by turning all mushy on him.

With all the passion and emotion bubbling around inside her, she held him tightly to her and kissed him fiercely until their breathing was ragged and aroused.

She arched against him, begging him to touch her. His hands explored her waist, her throat, her arms, and finally—

when she didn't think she could endure another moment of this exquisite tension—his fingers reached the summit of one breast.

For long moments he teased and touched and—blessed day!—finally worked her bra free so he could taste her.

His mouth was warm against her skin, and everything inside her shivered with delight that turned to aching hunger when he drew her into his mouth, his teeth gently scraping her flesh.

She wanted to hold him to her forever, to wrap her arms around him and never let go.

Tension spiraled higher as they explored curves and hollows. Soon they removed the last few scraps of clothing between them. With tantalizing gentleness, his fingers brushed between her thighs and her body cried out for more.

Every nerve cell seemed alive, vibrant, aching. She felt like a tightly strung wire, humming and buzzing and ready to snap.

At long last he knelt above her and entered her. Taylor held him tightly, trying to choke down the words of love bubbling through her. *Not now.*

He cared about her. She sensed it in the heat of his kiss, that tenderness in his eyes, but she couldn't burden him with a love he didn't return. She wouldn't. Maybe the day would come when she could let it out, but for now she would hold her love safely inside her.

He moved slowly at first—long, deep movements that left her trembling, weak, aching. Nothing existed but their joined bodies, their clenched hands, their tangled mouths.

When she thought she would break apart from this unbearable tension, he reached between them to slide his fingers across the aching center of her desire.

She gasped out his name as her release engulfed her in hot,

drenching waves. He kissed her fiercely, swallowing each sound of arousal, then with a ragged cry he found his own release.

"I missed class," she murmured moments later, after they both came back to earth and found themselves tangled together on his bed with afternoon sunlight streaming through the window.

"Sorry," he murmured, though the word was the most bald-faced lie he'd ever uttered.

"You are not," she accused.

"Are you?"

He was asking more than whether she regretted playing hooky, he realized as he held his breath, awaiting her reply.

She kissed his shoulder, the nearest body part to her mouth. "No," she said, then he felt the tickle of her facial muscles twisting into one of those rare smiles. "I hate that class."

"Anytime you want to ditch it, just let me know."

"You're a bad influence, Wyatt McKinnon. You were probably one of those mad, bad, dangerous boys all the girls were crazy about."

His laugh was rueful. "In my dreams, maybe. In reality, I was a shy, awkward geek who could barely remember my own name when I was in the presence of a pretty girl."

He still wasn't much better. For a man who made his living with words, he couldn't seem to find the right ones to tell Taylor how moving he found what they had just shared. He wanted to tell her how much he had come to care about her, but everything he started to say tangled in his throat. Inside, he was still that ungainly kid, all bony elbows and knobby knees and social awkwardness.

"I'm very glad you're not shy anymore," she said softly.

She pressed her mouth to the hollow of his neck and to his

considerable surprise, his body responded instantly, as if he were that teenager again.

"Not shy at all," she said with an arch look as she noticed his renewed vigor.

They made love again, this time more slowly, playfully. The laughter faded when he entered her again, replaced by an aching tenderness that shook him to his core.

"You must be starving," he murmured hours later, when the sun's shadows on the bed had lengthened.

"I haven't had a lot of time to think about my stomach."

"I have. And your legs and your shoulders and all the really fun spots in between."

She laughed. "What time is it?"

He squinted at his alarm clock. "Looks like it's almost five. Why don't we have a shower and then I'll take you somewhere for dinner. Or better yet, we can order in."

"If I get in that shower with you, it will be morning before we find anything to eat."

His laugh was husky and thrummed down her spinal cord like the plucked string of a violin. "You're probably right," he said. "How about you shower, and I'll round us up something to eat?"

"Can you cook?"

He shook his head. "Sorry. I can do scrambled eggs but that's about it. I'm afraid cooking is not one of my skills, although I have been told I compensate in other areas."

I'll just bet you have, she thought. "*You* shower, and I'll find us something besides eggs to eat. I'll shower after the water heats up again."

He agreed, although not without complaining about the wasted energy they would expend with two showers. In truth,

Taylor was grateful for a moment away from him so she could find her balance again.

Making love with him hadn't been among her best decisions, she acknowledged ruefully when she was alone in his small but efficient kitchen.

It had been wonderful—intense and passionate and tender. And fun. She had never realized intimacy could be so much fun. Their time together was something she would treasure for the rest of her life. But she greatly feared her heart would never recover.

If only things could be different between them. He cared about her, she knew that, but he didn't love her—not as she loved him. Already she could feel her heart brace itself for the inevitable pain.

She rubbed at the heavy ache in her chest. What a tangled mess.

With a sigh, she turned her attention to food. She opened his refrigerator to see what she could whip up. It was remarkably well stocked for the second home of a bachelor who couldn't cook. She wondered if he had a service or something to take care of it, because she had a tough time picturing the sexy and rugged Wyatt McKinnon she knew comparing melons in the supermarket.

Something quick and easy, she decided, settling on pasta.

She was mixing together a basic cream sauce when the phone rang. She could hear the shower still going and paused, undecided about whether to answer. Before she could make up her mind, the ringing stopped and she realized a fax was coming through on the phone/fax unit in the kitchen.

Whatever he was receiving was none of her business, she thought, and added peas and diced yellow squash to the sauce. She would have stuck to her conviction to mind her own business except that the cupboard containing glassware was just above the fax machine.

When she reached inside for a couple of wineglasses, her gaze fell on the paper in the fax machine and somehow lit on the one name she wouldn't have expected to see.

Kate Spencer.

Taylor nearly dropped the wineglasses. She fumbled and caught them just in time, then, with a furtive look at the bathroom door, picked up the two-page transmission.

She got no farther than the first page, which she discovered was a letterhead for something called St. Claire Investigations. She scanned it quickly.

"Hey, McKinnon," the cover letter read. "Here's the information you wanted about subject Kate Spencer. I'm dumping you everything I can find. Judging by her driver's license photo, she's a real looker. I can see why the interest. Let me know what else you need."

It was signed by someone named Dooley St. Clair.

Taylor stared at the paper in her hands so hard the lines began to blur.

Wyatt had a private investigator looking into Kate's background! It was all here in black and white. She turned the page and saw Kate's history in the foster system—not particulars, just dates and places. How she changed her name at eighteen from Katie Golightly to Kate Spencer, the last name of the foster parents who had given her love and nurturing. High school graduation, her college scholarship information, a speeding ticket she received near Pensacola—it was all there.

Why?

Why on earth would Wyatt investigate Kate? She closed her eyes as emotions assailed her. All she could see with her eyes shut was that day in the restaurant, how Wyatt couldn't stop staring at Kate.

He was obsessed with her. But how could he make love to Taylor with such laughter and tenderness all afternoon when he knew he was running a background check on Kate?

She couldn't handle this today, not after what had happened with Martin. Oh, her stomach hurt.

How could one woman be so completely wrong about *two* men? This had to be some kind of record—betrayed twice in one day.

Only this hurt much worse than what Martin had done.

She couldn't seem to think rationally, could focus only on her need to escape. The shower stopped just then and she knew she probably only had a few moments. She turned off the gas on the stove, yanked on her clothes in record time and hurried out the door, stuffing her feet in her shoes as she ran.

By the time she drove past the pair of towering Douglas firs that guarded the driveway to the house in Little Cottonwood Canyon, the sun had nearly slipped behind the mountains and the raw pulsing pain in her heart had subsided to a dull, steady ache. Her eyes burned from the tears she refused to shed.

She hated thinking what a fool she'd been. She had been so desperate for someone to trust that she had ignored every single blasted red flag about Wyatt. She should have clued in at lunch that day and guarded her heart better. Instead, she had only fallen harder for the man, so hard she didn't know if she would be able to do anything but lie here on the ground winded and stunned.

It was all her own fault. She couldn't really blame him for what had happened earlier. She had come uninvited to his apartment, had basically thrown herself at him.

She had made the first move, kissing him as she had done. What was he supposed to do? Shove her out the door? *Thanks, but no thanks?*

At least she didn't have to face Kate yet. For the next few weeks her roommate was scheduled to work the night shift at the hospital and wouldn't be in until early morning.

Taylor wasn't sure she had the strength to treat Kate as if nothing had happened—which she knew was completely unfair to her friend. Kate had done absolutely nothing wrong. She was as much a victim in all of this as Taylor—more, really. Kate was the one whose privacy had been invaded, her background probed.

What was she going to tell Kate? she wondered. How could she find the words to tell her friend what Wyatt had done?

Taylor desperately craved a long soak in the tub. Oh, how she longed for her little house with the big clawfoot tub perfect for long bubble baths. Although this house had several comfortable jetted tubs, she still preferred her deep old-fashioned one.

To Taylor's surprise, Belle didn't come running when she unlocked the front door of the cabin and walked inside. Now, that was odd. She hadn't seen her in the fenced run outside that Hunter had built for the dog either. If Belle wasn't inside and she wasn't in the run, where else would Kate have left her?

She closed the door behind her, then heard frantic, muffled barking from somewhere in the house. What in the world? For one thing, Belle wasn't much of a barker. For another, she always rushed to the door the moment she heard it open, no matter where she was.

More baffled than worried, Taylor followed the sound to the small bathroom off the kitchen. The closer she got to the room, the more frantic the barking became. It sounded as if

Belle was standing on her hind legs against the door, whining and scratching with her forelegs, something so unlike her that Taylor had to wonder if the dog was sick, if maybe that was why Kate had left her shut inside the bathroom.

No, Kate would never have left an ill creature. She would have called in sick to work herself before leaving Belle alone.

"What are you doing in there, you crazy dog. How did you manage to lock yourself in the bathroom? Come on, let's get you out of there." She reached to open the door, bracing herself to unleash seventy pounds of agitated canine. Before she could pull it open, though, she sensed movement from the hall to her left.

She blinked, totally stunned when Martin James walked into the hallway.

Taylor dropped her hand from the door and pressed it to her chest, where her heart seemed to stutter in shock. "Martin! You scared me! What are you doing here?"

"What do you say we leave the dog where she is for now?" He stepped closer and, oddly, Taylor fought the urge to take a step back.

"You put her in there?"

"That bitch already took one chunk out of me tonight. I'm not in the mood to be her chew toy."

She didn't know what shocked her more, his sudden jarring appearance in her kitchen, his angry tone, or the jagged rip in his black slacks.

For some strange reason, her brain decided to focus on that. "Belle bit you? That's impossible! She's the most gentle dog imaginable."

"Tell that to my plastic surgeon while he's sewing up the three-inch bite mark on my leg."

Taylor finally registered how odd it was to find Martin

James in her kitchen. "Did Kate let you in before she left for work? What are you doing here?"

"Waiting for you," he answered.

She wasn't sure why those words seemed to chill her blood.

Though she had a hard time mustering it in light of Wyatt's more recent—and more painful—betrayal, she gathered her anger around her. "I'm not sure I want to talk to you," she said bluntly. "No matter what you say, you're still fired. Hunter needs a lead attorney who believes unconditionally in his innocence. I think it should be obvious to both of us that attorney is not you."

He continued watching her with that odd expression on his face. "I'm not here to talk about your brother."

Taylor decided she was sick of men playing games with her today. She was tired and confused and wanted to nurse her heartbreak by herself. "Then what? Whatever it is, can we get on with it? It's been a long and difficult day and I'm not really in the mood for a confrontation."

He stepped closer, sparking more wild scrabbling by Belle on the other side of the door. "You brought this on yourself. Remember that."

Who was this man? He didn't look at all like the kindly Martin she had known all her life. He looked hard, distant. Dangerous, even.

"You couldn't leave it alone, could you," he said in a flat tone. "I had a messy problem but I managed to wrap it up in a tidy little package. It would have stayed wrapped up, but you wouldn't let it go, you just had to keep tugging and tugging on the strings."

Nervousness was beginning to filter through her exhaustion. Still, she tried to reason it away. This was Martin. He wouldn't hurt her.

"I'm too tired to figure out what you're talking about and I need to let Belle out."

"The dog stays where she is. And I'm afraid you and I need to take a walk."

She opened her mouth to tell him she wasn't going anywhere, that she'd had enough and he would have to leave now. But any words she wanted to form died in her throat when she spied the gun in his hand.

Chapter 15

Taylor stared at the gun, her heart fluttering in her chest.

How could this be happening? This was Martin, her father's friend. Someone who had until today always been kind to her.

Why was he holding a gun on her?

As if sensing her sudden fear, Belle barked louder and scratched against the door. A second later the door vibrated on its hinges, Belle throwing herself against it.

"Easy, Belle," she called out softly, afraid the dog would hurt herself. It was a good reminder. *Take it easy.* She could figure something out. She was smart, she was young, she was strong.

Of course, that evil-looking gun in Martin's hand trumped any advantage she might have.

"If that dog doesn't settle down, I'll shoot her," Martin warned, steel in his voice.

"Why?" Taylor's voice sounded hollow, thready.

"Because she's annoying me."

"No, why are you standing in my kitchen holding a gun on me? If you're going to shoot me, I at least deserve to know why."

"I'm not going to shoot you," Martin said calmly. "Shooting you would be messy and would raise too many questions. I learned my lesson with Dru and Mickie. I'm afraid you're going to have a little accident. Poor thing, you went for an evening hike and tumbled off a cliff. Or at least that's what it will look like. No suspicious circumstances, no unfortunate questions from the police. Just a tragedy all the way around."

Taylor almost didn't register the grim message in his words. Fear spurted through her, icy cold and relentless. He planned to kill her—just as he had killed Dru and her mother.

Part of her couldn't believe it, but when she looked at his face she saw something hard, something *empty.* "You shot those women." It was a statement, not a question, and earned her a glare.

"I had to. I didn't want to, any more than I want to hurt you. But Mickie had your same brand of dogged determination. She wouldn't leave well enough alone. When she wouldn't listen to reason, she really gave me no alternative."

I'll listen to reason, she wanted to cry. *I'll listen to whatever you want to say, as long as you don't kill me.*

If she thought begging might help, she would certainly try it, but this man she thought she had known all her life was a stranger. Somehow she didn't think even her most ardent, impassioned plea would persuade him to spare her life.

"Mickie was dying," Martin said, his tone biting, "and she wanted to absolve her conscience by coming clean. I tried to explain to her that spilling everything might purge *her* conscience, but it would leave the rest of us twisting in the wind long after her death. Who knows, maybe the chemo fried her brain or something, but the stupid bitch wouldn't listen."

"Is this about the Valencia case?" she asked. If she could distract Martin with questions, maybe she could figure out some way to escape.

"Poor Paul Valencia. Bastard never had a chance. You should have left well enough alone too, Taylor. Then you wouldn't be in this mess. You were getting too close, though, and I knew this morning, when you came to my office with that Valencia file, that I would have to stop you."

Belle renewed her violent efforts to get free and Taylor held her breath, afraid Martin would follow through on his threat to shoot the dog. Instead he pointed the gun at her.

"I'll explain everything while we're taking our lovely moonlit stroll. Let's walk."

"I'm not wearing shoes for hiking. Don't you think that will raise questions?"

He stared at her slick-soled loafers for a moment, then gave a low curse. "All right. Change into hiking boots, then."

That accomplished little except to delay the inevitable, she thought a few minutes later when she walked out into the cold mountain air. But a few minutes seemed a gift when her life was ticking away.

"Which way?" she asked, her voice roughened by fear and strain.

Martin gestured to the steep trail that cut through pine and aspen as it switchbacked up the mountainside. Her heart sank. Either Martin had done his homework or he'd made a lucky guess. She had walked this trail often and knew there were a half-dozen places where a person could slip and fall to her death.

"Walk," he ordered.

Taylor thought about refusing and forcing him to shoot her

right here, messy or not, but she couldn't quite find the courage. Part of her still hoped that perhaps she could figure out some way to escape, and instinct told her she would have a much better chance at it on the trail.

She set off up the mountainside with Martin close behind.

Any wild hope she might have entertained about outpacing him on the steep trail was quickly squashed when he kept up with her easily. Treadmill, she remembered. Despite his round physique, he and Judy had matching units in their bedroom and worked out faithfully.

She forced herself to slow her pace. No sense running to her own death. "If I'm going to die," she said, "at least I deserve to know why. Can you tell me what Mickie wanted to purge her conscience about? Was there some kind of irregularity in the trial proceedings?"

He snickered. "You could say that."

"What kind of irregularity?"

Like every other attorney or attorney-in-training she'd met, Martin seemed eager to talk. "I guess you know something about the case?"

She nodded. "A little. I've just read some media coverage and what was in the appellate court report. I haven't finished the complete transcript of court proceedings."

"You've probably read enough to know the rape and murder of little Jenny Monroe had the whole state in an uproar," he said. "The people wanted justice for that poor little girl, no matter the cost. They wanted somebody to pay. Anybody."

"Paul Valencia."

"Right."

They were walking through a stand of pine trees, so thick and dark that the twilight waned here. It wasn't full dark but it was hard to see in the dim light and she almost stumbled over a rock half-buried on the trail. She caught herself but the near fall sparked an idea she decided to nurture until the time was right.

"Valencia was in the wrong place at the wrong time," Martin continued. "He was no saint, had two priors, but they were for robberies. What convicted him was his fingerprint found in that little girl's bedroom. Of course, they could have been left there when he was paid to install some bathroom cabinets for her parents a few weeks before the kidnapping."

"He wasn't guilty," she surmised.

"We all thought he was. If for one moment anybody had thought he was innocent, none of it would have happened."

"What wouldn't have happened?"

They were both breathing hard by this time as the trail continued to climb, and he didn't answer her immediately. If she could keep him talking, she thought, perhaps he wouldn't notice this would be a logical spot for a twilight hiker to fall to her death.

"What did Mickie have to do with the case?"

"She worked for the prosecuting attorney's office. She's the one who brokered the deal."

In this context, the word sounded ominous. "Deal?"

"I was young, struggling. A public defender with no money and no reputation. The county prosecutor wanted this one put to bed quickly. I agreed to help them, in exchange for a fee and for select favors to be specified later."

"You threw the case."

"The evidence wasn't strong against Valencia. I just helped it along some. A misfiled brief here, an alibi witness discredited there. All subtle and all virtually undetectable but enough to do the job."

The implications—such gross, flagrant abuse of the judicial system—chilled her. "When did you all realize Valencia wasn't guilty?"

"When three other little girls were murdered in California in exactly the same manner while Valencia was awaiting his execution date. It was too early for DNA in those days but, funny thing. Turns out fingerprints from the California crime scenes matched unidentified prints also found in little Jenny Monroe's bedroom."

"You were his defense attorney.. That should have made your day."

"You'd think. But this case was different. California didn't even have a suspect. We had a bird all ready to be plucked."

"An innocent bird!"

"You didn't know the mood of the public at the time," he answered, panting as they continued their ascent. "There would have been a huge outcry if Valencia walked free. The parties involved all decided we'd be better off to let this one ride."

Dismay and horror churned through her. "You let an innocent man be executed! How could you have done that?"

"Believe me, no one was happy about it, but what else could we do? By that point it was too late to go back. For thirty years we'd lived with it. Mickie was dying, though, and she wanted to come clean. She didn't care that in her quest for atonement, she would have destroyed the rest of us."

"So you killed her."

"I didn't plan to," Martin answered, in what he probably thought was a reasonable tone. "I went over to talk some sense into her, but she wouldn't listen to reason. Things started to get a little loud and a little physical when Dru came in with a gun."

"Hunter's gun."

"Yeah, Hunter's gun. Lucky break for me. I knew at that

point I would have do something. As Valencia's defense counsel, I was most culpable for what we had let happen. I would have been destroyed—disbarred at the very least, most likely arrested. My reputation destroyed, everything I had worked for... I couldn't let Mickie ruin everything I had spent my whole life building. It was easy enough to take the gun from a pregnant woman."

She shivered from the cold, dispassionate way he described killing two women and a fetus. How could such evil lurk inside someone she had known all her life? Someone who had been close friends with her father, someone she and Hunter had both trusted with his life?

A lucky break, he had said about Dru coming in with Hunter's weapon. He must have known Hunter would be a logical suspect in the murders of Dru and her mother. Everyone knew her brother's relationship with Dru had been a stormy one, and despite his record on the police force, she knew he had enemies in the department who had been all too willing to believe him capable of murder.

She'd learned enough in two years of law school to know how a corrupt attorney could taint the judicial process. As Martin had said, it could be as easy as a misfiled brief.

Despite the fear pulsing through her veins at the gravity of her situation, she was aware of a deep, throbbing anger. Because of Martin James, her brother had endured hell for the past thirty months. *She* had been through hell, had lost friends, a career she loved—her entire house, even.

The thought jolted her and she stopped in her tracks. "You burned down my house," she exclaimed.

He prodded her with the gun to keep going. "A distraction attempt that unfortunately didn't work. I was trying to frighten you off. The minute you started working with McKinnon, I knew the two of you would be trouble. I sent you a crime scene photo as a warning and, when that didn't work, I torched your house. You were supposed to be so distraught at finding yourself suddenly homeless that you wouldn't have the time or energy to work on the appeal. I didn't give enough credit to your stubbornness, though."

They had reached another steep part of the trail, so vertical that all Kate could see below her off the trail in the waning light was a carpet of treetops.

If he planned to do this before dark, he would have to move soon, she thought. Panic and terror gripped her, and it took all her concentration to keep from giving in to them. She didn't want to die here. She wanted to live to see this man brought to justice for what he had done to so many lives.

"So now what? To cover up your thirty-year-old crime, you're going to kill me…and then how many more? There are others who know as much as I do, who will be able to connect the dots after I'm dead."

"McKinnon? I've done my homework. I saw you two the night of the fire. He'll be so distraught after your death he'll forget all about an old murder case."

She almost corrected him but decided to leave the man his illusions. If Martin succeeded in murdering her, she knew Wyatt wouldn't be distraught. Oh, she knew he wouldn't be cold and dispassionate about her death—he would probably mourn her as a friend, someone he cared about—but he wouldn't let his mourning distract him from the book.

She could find comfort from that, she decided. Wyatt would continue looking for the truth after she was dead.

No, she wasn't going to die, she vowed. She would fight, do everything she had to.

"This is as good a spot as any," Martin said.

Whenever she walked Belle on this trail she tried to be cautious of the loose shale and treacherous footing. The mountain sheared off steeply on the other side of the trail, with a drop of at least two hundred feet.

If she were planning to shove someone over the side of the mountain, this would be a good spot…

The thought ricocheted through her mind. She could turn the tables on Martin. She found the idea horribly repugnant but knew she couldn't wholly reject it.

She had to do something. Was she strong enough, physically and emotionally, to take such a drastic step?

She had to save herself. That was the bottom line. She *had* to.

If she died here on this mountain, knowledge of Martin's crimes would die with her. Wyatt might continue looking for answers, but chances were good he would find nothing. If she died, no one would ever know that her brother had been framed by his own defense counsel.

Hunter would wither away in prison, dying by inches in that hellish place—until his execution ended it.

She had to do this. She had no choice. If she didn't, Martin would kill her and Hunter would be left with nothing.

Her mind raced furiously as her eyes did a careful sweep of her surroundings. She pretended to stumble with a ragged gasp. For a few heart-stopping seconds she slid on the loose shale a few feet closer to the edge, but as she had hoped, before she reached the point of no return she was able to wedge her foot under the looped root of a small clump of sagebrush. It wouldn't hold her for long and certainly wouldn't withstand extreme force, but she had to pray it would be enough.

"Too bad." Martin stepped closer, shaking his head. "A few more yards and your death really would have been an accident."

Her heart pounded in her ears with deafening force and she was trembling so much inside, she could hardly find words but she forced herself to speak. "I'm not going to make it easy for you," she snapped.

"It's not easy, Taylor."

To her amazement, he looked genuinely hurt.

"You can't believe that. This is the hardest thing I've ever done," he said.

She drew deep inside herself for calm. "If you want me to die on this mountain you're going to have to push me yourself. I want you to spend the rest of your life remembering this moment—the smell of the air and the wind ruffling your hair and the sound of my screams as I go over. I want you to watch me tumble to my death, remembering how you were always kind to me during my father's illness, how when I was a child you used to call me Strawberry Shortcake and always had a supply of English toffee in your pocket."

She paused and met his gaze squarely. "I want you to look in my eyes as you kill me and know this was no accident— and that someday you will pay for it."

"Very affecting closing argument, Counselor." There was genuine regret in his voice. "You would have been a hell of a trial attorney, even if you were only in it for your brother's sake. I'm almost sorry you won't get that chance."

He stepped closer, moving exactly where she needed him. "I don't have a choice here. You have to see that," he said.

"Neither do I," she whispered. Then, with a deep breath and a prayer of gratitude to Kate for dragging her to kick-boxing classes all summer, she dug her toes tighter under the root and kicked her free leg out with all her might. Her boot connected to his chest with shuddering force.

It all happened in an instant but time seemed to slow, to

drag on forever. He staggered backward, then started to slide on the loose shale. Martin raised the gun and for one heart-stopping moment Taylor stared at death, certain he would shoot her and end everything right here. And then his arms flew out and the gun landing harmlessly in the rocks as he tried to keep his balance.

He scrambled for purchase for what seemed like forever, but he was off balance and couldn't hang on. As she watched, horrified, he tumbled backward over the lip of the trail with a hoarse scream.

For several agonizing moments as he fell, she could hear nothing but that terrible, echoing cry. Then his body landed far below with a jarring, sickening thud.

Taylor sank to her knees, heedless of the sharp rocks gouging through her pants. Her breath came in high gasps and she had to shove her fists against her stomach to keep from retching.

Dear God. She had just killed a man.

What had she done?

The nausea overwhelmed her—her stomach was empty but that didn't stop her from dry-heaving into the rocks. She wiped her mouth and crouched there, dizzy and sick, until she heard a low, distant moan from far below.

He wasn't dead! At least not yet.

She could just make out a terrible gurgle, and then his voice—that smooth, well-modulated voice that could so easily hypnotize a jury—called to her, raw with pain.

"Taylor? Don't leave me here. Please don't leave me here."

She stared down into the darkness, all her medical training screaming at her to do something to ease his pain—the pain that she had caused.

If she tried to make it down that steep slope to him in the

gathering darkness, she would die right along with him, she realized. She needed to call search-and-rescue.

If Martin died from his injuries, she realized, no one would believe her story that he had confessed to killing Dru and Mickie, that he had rigged the Valencia trial, that he had tried to kill her. It would sound like the wild imaginings of a desperate woman.

"Hang on," she called down. "I'm going for help."

Chapter 16

Something was wrong.

Wyatt stood on the front porch of the Bradshaws' log and rock house in Little Cottonwood Canyon, not sure why his instincts hummed like juice through a bad power line.

Maybe he was imagining things. Maybe he was only upset that she had run away after the heat and tenderness they had shared. His heart still ached from coming out of the shower to find her gone.

He knew why she had left—it hadn't taken much sleuthing, especially after he found that damn report from Dooley St. Clair on the kitchen table. Too impatient to wait for the DNA report, he had asked a private investigator friend to run a cursory check on Kate, just to find basic information to rule out that family of identical siblings Gage had warned him about.

Taylor must have seen it as it came through or else it still would have been sitting in the fax machine. What kind of conclusion had she jumped to when she found out he'd run a background check on her friend and roommate?

He thought he had a pretty good idea, and he grimaced again. He would have to explain—to Taylor at the least, and by now she most likely had told Kate. He was going to have to explain things to her too.

If he had his way, he would wait another day or two to talk to Kate after the DNA tests came back, but the unfortunate timing of that fax had taken that decision out of his hands.

He had even delayed coming here long enough to try to track down Gage and see how soon they might know something, but he hadn't had any luck finding his brother.

Wyatt rang the doorbell again. He didn't want to tell either woman yet about his suspicions, but that didn't explain the unease he felt now.

Why wasn't she answering her door? He could see Taylor's car out front, though he was slightly relieved to see no sign of Kate's little Honda. He supposed they could have gone somewhere together in Kate's car, but something told him that wasn't the case.

He could hear Belle barking inside somewhere, as hyper as she'd been the day of the fire.

The memory stopped him cold.

The dog didn't bark much, Taylor had told him. So why was Belle in there howling as if every cat in the whole state was wandering through her territory?

He knocked one more time, then decided to try the door. To his further worry, it opened easily.

"Taylor?" he called out, only to be met by the sound of more frenzied barking. "Tay?"

He followed the sounds the dog was making and realized Belle was shut in a bathroom off the kitchen. The moment he opened the door, she raced to the outside door, snarling and barking.

What the hell?

He let her outside and the dog immediately took off through the moonlit night toward a steep trail that climbed the mountain through the evergreens behind the house.

His worry deepened. He thought about going back to check the house one more time, just to make sure Taylor wasn't lying hurt somewhere, unable to answer him, but he quickly discarded that idea. Belle never would have left the house if Taylor was inside in jeopardy. She would have rushed to her mistress's side—just as she was trying to do now.

No, Taylor was up there somewhere. He didn't know why she had taken off in the dark for a hike without her dog, but he knew without a doubt he would find her.

Though everything in him urged haste, he decided to err on the side of caution. He went to his Tahoe to find a few emergency supplies—a flashlight, a knife and a shiny silver survival blanket, just in case she was hurt in some way.

He had to hope he could catch up to Belle on the trail, or that Taylor hadn't strayed from it. With his heart pumping, he took off up the trail, moving as fast as he dared through a heavy darkness lit only by the pale moonlight and the beam of his flashlight.

He was just beginning to think he was crazy to be doing this when he thought he heard a dog's snuffling and then a crash on the switchback above him. He picked up his pace until he reached the spot where the trail turned. There ahead of him, he saw movement on the trail, and an instant later his flashlight beam picked up Taylor, with Belle stuck to her side like a burr.

"Who's there?" she called out, sounding panicked, and he realized the beam of the flashlight must be blinding her.

"It's me," he answered, moving quickly until he reached her. He pulled her into his arms. She was trembling, he realized, like a dry leaf about to fall. "What the hell are you doing up here?"

She sagged against him, her body going boneless. "Oh, Wyatt. You're here!" she said, and the simple, heartfelt gratitude in her voice just about knocked him to his knees.

Her arms twined around his waist and she held tight, her face buried in his shirt. "I'm so glad to see you. I can't even tell you how glad."

She was breathing hard and she sounded like she was teetering on the brink of hysteria.

"What's going on, Taylor? What are you doing up here?"

"I thought I was going to die, that I would never see you again. I *hated* thinking I would never see you again."

"I'm right here," he said. "Now tell me what's happened."

She stared at him in the moonlight, until Belle brushed against them, and then she seemed to blink back into awareness. She pulled away, that panic back in her eyes.

"Martin! I have to get help."

He didn't understand any of this. "Martin James? What is he doing up here?"

She didn't answer him, just pulled out of his arms and rushed down the mountainside, Belle inches from her side.

Wyatt stared after her for just a moment before taking off behind her. Maybe she slipped up there somehow and conked her head. What else would explain her strange behavior?

"Taylor! Tell me what's going on."

"I will. Just not yet. I need to call for help," she said.

Inside the house, she headed straight for the telephone. He followed her, growing more and more concerned. Her clothes were covered in dirt, the knees ripped, and she looked like she'd just been in a bar fight.

"I need to report a fall victim in Little Cottonwood Canyon, about a mile and a quarter up the Lupine Trail," she said after she dialed the emergency number. The wild panic from the trail was gone, as if it had never existed, replaced by a calm professionalism.

"Fifty-eight-year-old male in generally good condition sustained massive injuries from a fall of possibly seventy-five to a hundred feet. Search-and-rescue will need to lift him out and he will need immediate medical attention, probably LifeFlight."

She was silent for a moment, listening. "No, he was too far down the mountainside for me to assess his injuries personally, but from what I could see, he looked as if he had possible head injuries as well as multiple lacerations and broken bones. He was conscious when I left him, but that was fifteen to twenty minutes ago."

She was quiet for a moment again, then gave the dispatcher more detailed information about how to find the trailhead, and her phone number and address.

"Yes. I'll stay on the line until rescuers arrive," she said.

"What's going on, Tay?" he asked again, when it was obvious she'd been put on hold. "Why were you and Martin out there in the dark? How did he fall?"

"He had a gun. He made me go with him." The panic that had receded during the emergency call flowed back into her features and her eyes looked huge, haunted.

"And he didn't fall," she said, gripping the phone tightly. "I pushed him."

All the shock and horror of the last half hour surged back and her knees went weak, her head woolly. She might have fallen if Wyatt hadn't reached for her.

"I was so scared, Wyatt. I didn't know what to do. Martin killed Dru and Mickie. He admitted it to me."

She swayed again and Wyatt growled a curse. "You need to sit down," he ordered.

"I can't. I need to stay on the line, then show search-and-rescue where to find him."

"They're not here yet and probably won't make it up the canyon for another ten minutes or so. There's nothing you can do for him until then. Just take it easy for a minute."

She knew he was right, although it made her crazy that despite her medical training she was not able to help Martin—and that she was the one who had caused his injuries in the first place.

"Outside. I'll sit on the porch so we can watch for the rescue workers," she insisted.

He looked as if he wanted to argue but finally nodded. On the way out, he grabbed a fleece blanket from the couch and wrapped it around her shoulders. He sat on the porch swing, then pulled her—blanket, cordless phone and all—onto his lap.

The air was cold, bracing, and that along with the strength of his arms helped clear the lingering shock from her system.

"Tell me again. Why were you up there?"

"Martin wanted to kill me. He had a gun but he said he didn't want to shoot me—he wanted it to look like an accident, unlike the mess he made with Dru and Mickie. That's what he said, Wyatt. They were a mess he had to clean up and he did it by framing Hunter for the murder. As defense counsel, it was pitifully easy for him to ensure a conviction."

The same emotions she had felt at learning the truth chased across his features—shock and disbelief and fury.

"Why kill you?"

"The same reason he killed Dru and Mickie—I threatened

the safe little world he'd created. When I went to his office today, I made the mistake of asking him about the Valencia case. That's what this is all about, a thirty-year-old murder trial. He must have panicked when I brought it up. Even though we hadn't put all the pieces together yet, he couldn't run the risk that we would."

While they waited for rescue workers, he held her while she poured out the whole story, everything she had learned since walking into the cabin after leaving his ranch.

"Mickie wanted absolution, I guess," she said after she finished. "She didn't want to die with an innocent man's death on her conscience. All she wanted was a little peace, and he killed her for it."

"Poor Dru."

"Right. With all the many people who might have wanted her out of the picture—John Randall, those she would have implicated in her police corruption story—she ended up being killed only because she tried to protect her dying mother."

His arms tightened around her and they sat in silence until they heard the wail of sirens that heralded the arrival of rescue workers.

Though she was still shaky and exhausted, Taylor insisted on hiking back up with the rescue crew to locate the spot where Martin had slipped. As Wyatt refused to let her out of his sight, he went along too.

She was grateful for his support, she had to admit. Hiking back up that trail was one of the hardest things she'd ever had to do, emotionally and physically. With every step, she seemed to replay that horrible moment when Martin tumbled over the side.

What if he was dead? Even after everything he had done,

she couldn't bear to think about someone lying broken and bleeding and dying alone on that mountainside.

Not when she had been the one to put him there.

By the time they reached the shale bed, her stomach churned and she prayed she wouldn't be sick again, especially when they were greeted at the spot by only a vast, terrible silence.

While a team of rescue workers set up ropes to rappel down the mountain, Taylor waited anxiously for news, her hands clenched together.

She nearly sagged to the ground when the two paramedics who had gone down to him reported back via walkie-talkies that Martin had a pulse—weak, but there—and was semiconscious.

It took rescuers nearly thirty minutes to load him into the stretcher and hoist him up the mountainside. Though Wyatt tried to convince her to go back down to the house and get out of the way of the recovery, Taylor insisted on staying. She had to see him for herself, to make sure he would survive to pay the price for his sins.

He had already paid in part, she acknowledged when he was pulled onto the trail in the stretcher. He was battered and bloody, his face nearly unrecognizable from the lacerations and his arm bent at an awkward angle.

She had done this to him, she thought. Yet she couldn't be sorry. If she hadn't somehow found the courage, she would be the one on the stretcher—or worse, she would be lying on that mountainside dead or dying.

"Strawberry Shortcake," he mumbled when he saw her, out of lips that were swollen to twice their normal size. "So sorry. Guess I went a little crazy."

Her mouth tightened. *A little crazy* implied one-time, aberrant behavior. This went far beyond that. Martin had spent thirty years covering his tracks—to do it, he had taken two lives. No, she corrected. Four, counting Paul Valencia and Dru's unborn baby.

He had been ready to kill her and let Hunter die by lethal injection, after her brother spent who knows how long in that hell of a prison.

No, it would be a long time before she could feel any sympathy for Martin James.

After she watched the rescue workers start their trek down the mountain with Martin's stretcher, Taylor turned back to Wyatt.

"Thank you for coming up with me. It helped."

"You're looking pale. Are you sure you can make it back down?"

The concern in his voice warmed her just as surely as that fleece blanket he had tucked around her earlier. Still, she had to wonder what kind of game he was playing. She wished she could trust her own instincts, could believe he was just as caring and tender as he seemed. Every time she let herself lean on him, though, she remembered that fax about Kate.

"I'll be fine. I just want to go home."

He nodded and led the way down the trail.

When they returned to the house, she found the county sheriff's deputy waiting to talk to her about Martin's injuries and about the events leading up to them.

While she spent two grueling hours giving them her statement, apparently Wyatt found plenty to occupy himself.

He lit a fire in the massive great room fireplace to take the lingering chill out of the air, ordered enough pizza to feed an army—and must have paid a small fortune to have it delivered this far up the canyon—and took time in between to make a few phone calls of his own.

One of those calls resulted in the arrival of a tall, dark-haired man in jeans and a leather jacket, who showed up just after the deputies finished their pizza and left.

"This is Nick Sinclair, a friend of mine," Wyatt explained, and Taylor blinked, recognizing the name if not the man himself.

Sinclair was one of the most prominent criminal defense attorneys west of the Mississippi, with a reputation that exceeded Martin's. He would have been her second choice to defend her brother—her first, if not for Martin's connection to the family—but she knew how difficult it was to even talk to the man on the phone.

What kind of strings must Wyatt have pulled?

"I knew you would want to set the wheels in motion to free Hunter as soon as possible," Wyatt said. "When I explained the situation, Nick was eager to help."

She didn't know what to say. Nick Sinclair lived on a vast private ranch in Wyoming, she knew. Wyatt must have moved heaven and earth to get him here so quickly.

To her dismay, tears welled up in her eyes and she tried to choke them back, unwilling to let this stranger see how much Wyatt's actions had touched her.

At her silence, Wyatt started to look a little uncomfortable. "You can pick a different attorney of your own if you want, but Nick might be able to at least help you figure out what hoops you'll have to jump through to get Hunter out as soon as possible."

"Oh, thank you," she exclaimed. She decided she didn't care what some strange attorney thought of her—she threw her arms around Wyatt's neck and kissed him fiercely.

"You're very welcome," he murmured against her mouth.

Then, with reluctance in his eyes, he turned her over to Sinclair for a consultation.

For the next hour, she and the attorney discussed strategy. She knew it would take time to free her brother—the saying about the wheels of justice grinding slowly was an old one, but unfortunately also a true one. A judge would have to void his conviction based on new evidence, something that couldn't happen overnight.

But at least those wheels were in motion, she thought as she showed Nick Sinclair out. At least the terrible fear she had lived with for nearly three years would soon be only a memory.

After he left, the adrenaline surge that had carried her through the long, difficult evening seemed to abate in an instant. She walked into the great room, conscious of two things—that every muscle in her body ached and that she and Wyatt were alone for the first time since rescuers had arrived at the cabin hours earlier.

She found him sitting on the couch in front of the fire, Belle at his feet and a pen and paper in his hand as he wrote, and she fell in love with him all over again.

Her sexy cowboy scholar, she thought, then winced as her heart gave a quick spasm. No. Not hers. She might want him to be—but what she wanted and what she was likely to get were two completely different things.

Still, when he realized she was standing there, he set whatever he was writing aside and held out his arms.

Though she knew it was foolish of her and would only delay her inevitable heartbreak, at that moment she wanted nothing more than the safe harbor he offered.

Taylor settled into his arms with a sigh that sounded as if it came from the depths of her toes.

She was too pale, he thought, concerned. Her eyes still had those dark, haunted shadows and she looked as if she would fall over if he opened the window to let in a breeze.

"How did it go with Nick?" he asked.

"Good. He thinks Hunter might be out within the week. Can you believe that? Even if Martin recants what he told me, Mr. Sinclair seemed to think it likely the unidentified partial on the gun will be traced to him, and that the eyewitness who saw a vehicle leave the murder scene could positively identify Martin's vehicle. Added to my testimony about what he told me and his actions tonight, that should be enough for an indictment."

"Good. It's going to make a hell of a book. I wonder if Martin will give me a jailhouse interview."

She made a sound that could have been a rough laugh, but all he heard through it was her exhaustion.

"Thank you for being here tonight," she said. "I would like to think I could have handled things without you, but I'm so glad I didn't have to. You made everything easier."

"I didn't do anything." He couldn't seem to keep the bitterness from his words. "I should have been here to protect you."

"How could you? You didn't know Martin would come here. You didn't even know *I* was coming here."

At that, her mouth tightened, and in her eyes he saw the memory of the afternoon they had spent in each other's arms—and her mad dash from his apartment.

"Why did you leave?" he asked, although he was sure he already knew the answer.

She confirmed it. "I saw the fax you received about Kate. I wasn't snooping, I just happened to see it and I was…upset. I didn't know what to think."

That damn fax. He was going to have to talk to her about it, he realized, ready or not. "I figured that must have been it."

"I don't understand why you had a private investigator run a background check on Kate. I'd like to."

He sighed. "Can you trust me, just for a little while longer? I want to tell you everything but I just don't think I can yet."

A jumble of emotions played across her lovely fine-boned features. Confusion and doubt and uncertainty. Finally she nodded. "Okay."

He had a feeling she never would have let the matter drop if not for the fatigue he could see clouding her eyes, weighing down her shoulders.

"You need to get some rest, Tay. Come on. I'll tuck you in."

She was silent for so long, he thought maybe she had already fallen asleep. When she spoke, her voice was low, so quiet he could barely hear her.

"Will you stay, Wyatt? Kate is working the graveyard shift at the hospital and I don't want to be alone tonight."

"I'm not going anywhere, sweetheart," he promised.

"Thank you," she murmured, and a moment later her breathing slowed as she slipped into sleep.

For a long time he sat on the couch and held her in his arms while the fire burned down and the wind rattled dry leaves against the glass.

They would have to talk soon—and not only about Kate. At some point, he knew he had to talk to Taylor about his feelings for her. He had started to that afternoon when he was wrapped around her, inside her, but the words had clogged in his throat.

He had been running from those feelings as long as he'd known her, he recognized now, especially in the past month that they'd been working together on her brother's case.

He had thrown up barrier after barrier between them—her brother, the book he was writing, the threat to his objectivity—but now, in the honesty of the night, he admitted the truth.

He was scared, pure and simple.

Something about Taylor Bradshaw made him feel like the awkward nerdy kid he'd been at nine.

He had worked so hard after Charley had been taken to become as strong as Gage. He had worked out, lifted weights, started running. He had never built up much bulk—he just didn't have the metabolism for it—but at least he had turned what he had into powerful muscles.

Toughness. That had been the secret. If he could be tough enough—mentally and physically—he could make sure nothing so horrible, so out of his control could ever happen to him again. He never wanted to experience that terrible sense of vulnerability he had felt when he realized Charley was gone, so he had carefully built walls around his heart.

He cared about his family—his mom, his dad, Gage, and now Allie and her girls—but he refused to let anything else inside.

Maybe that was how he was able to write the things he did— because he never allowed any of the ugliness to touch him.

Taylor reached inside, though. From the very first time he saw her she had been sneaking through those defenses.

She threatened that veneer of strength he had worked so hard to build and made him feel like he was a child again, like the world was an exciting, terrifying, *wonderful* place.

He loved her.

His arms tightened around her as the truth settled in his chest. It wouldn't do him any good to run, because she would always be right there in his heart. If something had happened to her, if Martin had carried out the terrible crime he had intended, Wyatt didn't know how he would have survived.

He loved her, and he meant what he said to her before she fell asleep—he wasn't going anywhere.

Chapter 17

Taylor awoke to the smell of coffee, sunlight streaming through the wide bank of windows and a warm tongue in her ear. Her eyes reluctantly lifted and she moaned when she found Belle two inches from her face.

"Ugh. Dog germs," she muttered, using a corner of her quilt to wipe at her ear. "Go away, Belle."

"Sorry." A deep male voice jerked her the rest of the way out of sleep.

She turned her gaze to the doorway, where she found Wyatt leaning against the door frame, a steaming, spatterware mug in his hands and an odd expression in his eyes.

"I told her to let you sleep," he said, "but she wouldn't listen. She rushed right in here the minute my back was turned."

"It's all right." Her voice sounded raspy with sleep and she cleared the cobwebs out. "I needed to get up anyway. What time is it?"

"Eight-thirty," he answered.

Her mind processed that data, then she sat up abruptly. "Oh no! I have a nine a.m. class on Wednesdays. I'll never make it."

She scrambled to her feet in a panic, then with a jolt remembered the events of the night before—Martin, the mountain, his confession, everything—and she sagged back down to the sofa.

"I think you could take the day off from school—don't you, Counselor?" he asked. "Or the week. While we're at it, why don't you take the whole semester off and just go back to finish medical school spring semester?"

She closed her eyes. *Med school.* If Hunter really was going to be released, she could go back and finish her last few classes, then start her residency. She couldn't seem to comprehend it.

"I didn't dream everything last night, did I?"

"No. It's real."

He walked into the room and sat down, his features suddenly solemn. "I called the hospital this morning and Martin's been upgraded from critical to serious. He's got a long road ahead of him but he's expected to pull through, so he can face charges of attempted murder for what he tried to do to you—and who knows what other charges the prosecutor will come up with for the rest of it."

"Will he go to prison?"

"I think that's a given. At this point, I suppose, just a question of how long."

How would she face Judy? Taylor wondered. The poor woman would be devastated by everything her husband had done.

"Any word from Nick Sinclair about when Hunter will be able to come home?" she asked.

Wyatt laughed. "It's not even nine a.m., Taylor. The man is good but you'll have to give him a little time to work."

"I know. I'm just eager." She studied him, looking lean and gorgeous in the morning light. "I know I told you thank-you last night, but it's not enough. It will never be enough to let you know how grateful I am for everything you did."

He shook his head. "You're the one with the tenacity of a bulldog, who just kept shaking and shaking until you worked out the truth. I didn't do anything."

"You helped me when no one else would." She smiled at him. "You brought Nick Sinclair here. You stayed with me last night when I didn't want to be alone. Thank you."

At her words and her smile, his eyes darkened with some unreadable expression that sent her stomach fluttering, then he set his mug down on the coffee table and pulled her into his arms.

His kiss was tender and sweet and took her breath away, and she responded with all the emotion in her heart. They stood in that warm pool of morning sunlight for several long moments, their mouths tangled, and then he pulled away.

"Tay, I need to tell you something."

Her insides tightened at the seriousness of his tone. About Kate? she wondered, bracing herself, but before he could say anything Taylor heard the clink of a key in the front door lock.

A moment later, Kate let herself in. She was wearing scrubs, her blond hair was yanked back in a tight ponytail and her eyes were bleary from a twelve-hour night shift, but somehow she still managed to look lovely.

"What are you doing still here?" she asked Taylor, surprise in her blue eyes. "I thought you had class this morning. You're going to be late if you don't hurry."

Her gaze suddenly landed on Wyatt and those tired eyes

widened at finding him there so early. Taylor flushed at the speculation she saw leap into her friend's expression, fighting the urge to explain that things weren't what they appeared.

"Taylor's decided to skip her morning class in light of all she went through last night," Wyatt said.

To her dismay, he was staring at Kate as if he wanted to burn her image into his eyeballs—as if that emotional kiss he had just shared with Taylor had never existed.

Taylor's mind flashed on that fax, about the investigation he had run on Kate, and she thought her heart would shatter.

"What is he talking about?" Kate turned to her, concern on her face. "What did you go through?"

Oh, heavens! Kate knew nothing of what had happened, about Martin or his confession. She pushed away her heartbreak for now. "You're not going to believe it," she said, then told Kate the whole story.

By the time she finished Kate had sunk down onto a chair, her expression stunned. "So Hunter will be coming home?"

Taylor nodded, ecstatic all over again.

"Soon, we hope," Wyatt said, his gaze still glued to Kate. "Not overnight but soon."

"Incredible!" Kate exclaimed. "I can't believe I missed it all. You should have called me!"

"I'm sorry. Everything was so crazy last night, I didn't even think of calling you."

"This is amazing. I work one shift and come home to find that everything has changed."

Not *everything,* Taylor thought. She was still in love with a man who didn't return her feelings. As joyous as she was about Hunter, part of her heart grieved for what would never be.

The doorbell rang before *either* she or Wyatt could respond.

"I'll get that," Kate said. The exhaustion she had worn when she arrived home seemed to have disappeared amid the news about Hunter's imminent release. She hurried to the door.

A moment later, Taylor was surprised to see Kate usher in Gage McKinnon, looking handsome and dangerous in a dark gray suit.

What was it with these McKinnon men? Taylor wondered in disgust. The man had been married for only a few weeks, had a beautiful wife and two gorgeous little girls, but he couldn't take his eyes off Kate either.

"I heard about the excitement you had up here last night," Gage said to Wyatt, though his gaze never left Kate. "When I couldn't reach you at your apartment, I took a chance you'd still be here. And even if you weren't, I would have come up anyway."

Wyatt froze at his words, and Taylor watched as the brothers shared a look rich with layers of meaning, one she didn't understand.

"Is she?" Wyatt asked. He seemed to hold his breath as he waited for his brother's reply.

Gage looked first at Kate and then at his brother. "Looks like. The samples share both maternal and paternal DNA."

Wyatt made a move forward, then seemed to check himself. Both men continued staring at Kate, who was starting to look extremely uncomfortable at their attention.

She began edging out of the room. "Um, I have some things to do before I try to sleep a little, if you'll all excuse me."

"No!" Both men reached out as if to stop her, and Taylor decided she'd had enough.

"Wyatt, what is this about? Does this have something to do with the background check you ran on Kate?"

"What?" Kate exclaimed. "What background check?"

"Maybe you'd better sit down," Wyatt suggested. He

moved to Kate's side, staring down at her. "Hell, maybe *I'd* better sit down."

"Do you mind telling me what this is about?" Kate asked, the beginnings of anger in her voice. "What test are you talking about? What background check?"

Wyatt and Gage shared another long look. "Where do we start?" Wyatt asked.

Gage stepped forward. "This might help explain."

He held out a folder and opened it to reveal some photographs. The first one he pulled out was a picture of a woman in a dated wedding dress that could have been Kate at a costume party. He propped it up on the coffee table, and Kate looked at it, a baffled expression on her face.

"Who is this? I don't know this woman."

"Try this one," Gage said. He held out a family photo, and Taylor recognized Sam and Lynn McKinnon, two boys who had to be Gage and Wyatt, and a little blond girl with curls and a sweet smile.

"This is us with our little sister, Charlotte. She was kidnapped when she was three years old, about two months after that picture was taken," Gage said.

Gage set a third picture on the table. "And this is an age-progressed photograph we had an artist create a few years ago to show what Charlotte might look like today."

Taylor stared at it, speechless. Like the first picture Gage had presented, this one could have been a photograph of Kate—right down to the smile. Kate made a tiny gasping sound, then lowered herself into a chair. She looked as if Gage McKinnon had just plowed a fist in her gut.

"You think I'm this…this Charlotte?"

Gage shook his head. "No. We don't think anything. We know. We ran a DNA test from a sample Wyatt took when you had lunch together and compared it to his blood type. The two samples definitely share the same parentage. You're Charlotte."

The color leached from Kate's features, and for a moment Taylor was afraid her friend would pass out.

His sister! Wyatt was obsessed with Kate because he thought she was his missing *sister!* All the pieces of the puzzle seemed to click into place—his stunned expression at lunch, his probing questions into her childhood, the background check.

"You're wrong." Kate shook her head. "You have to be wrong. I...I wasn't kidnapped. It's impossible! Don't you think I would remember something like that? I don't remember! My mother's name is Brenda Golightly. I never knew my father but she said his name was Billy. She's all I can remember."

"You were only three when you were kidnapped, young enough that you probably don't have many memories of us," Gage said. "But that little girl in that picture is definitely you. You can run more DNA tests to prove it if you need corroboration—we'll do anything you want. But I can tell you right now, the results will be the same."

"How can this be—?" she asked, her voice cracking on the last word.

"I don't know," Wyatt said, and the joy on his face—on both their faces—was almost painful to see. "I only know that the moment you walked into that restaurant, I knew you had to be Charlotte. You look just like Lynn—our mother. *Your* mother."

"This is my...my mother?" Kate stared at the photograph of Lynn on what must have been her wedding day. She shifted her gaze to the family portrait of the five McKinnons. "And my father? I have a *father*?"

"And two brothers who love you," Wyatt said earnestly.

"Two brothers who never stopped looking for you, who never gave up hope that someday they would find you."

Taylor saw tears pooling in the corners of his eyes, and Gage's too, and emotion clogged her throat. These big, masculine men who walked the dark side of the human condition every day had just been handed a miracle. They looked like they would burst from happiness—and though Kate was still looking pale and shocked, Taylor knew when she had time to get used to the idea, she would come to love all the McKinnons.

Just as Taylor did…

"I couldn't tell you, Tay. I wanted to a hundred times but I didn't dare until I had proof."

A half hour later, Taylor returned downstairs after her quick shower—where, she had to admit, she had indulged in more weeping—to find the house quiet. Wyatt was sitting on the couch, still wearing that look of stunned joy. There was no sign of Gage or Kate.

"I had to be sure," Wyatt said. "I didn't want Kate to know anything until I had proof one way or the other, just in case I turned out to be delusional."

"I didn't know what to think when I saw that fax," she admitted. "Especially after we'd just made love."

"I should have told you."

"I thought—"

"I know what you must have thought," he murmured. "I'm sorry if you were hurt by it."

She flushed, embarrassed that she'd been so stupid. If she had paid attention, she would have seen the resemblance between Kate and Lynn. She remembered thinking that Wyatt's mother reminded her of someone, and now that the connection had been made, she couldn't believe she had missed it.

"Where is everyone?" she asked.

"Gage is taking Kate to meet Mom right now. The plan is that they'll call Sam when they get to Liberty so he can fly up from Las Vegas. Mom doesn't know anything of this. I hope it doesn't give her a heart attack when they show up like that."

"Don't you want to be there?"

"Yes." He paused, then knew he couldn't delay telling her any longer, despite the nerves jumping around inside him. "But I want you to come with me."

Her eyes widened. "Me? I don't belong with your family right now at such a joyful reunion. All I am is Kate's roommate."

"I hope you know you're more than that—to Kate and to me."

Other than taking a quick breath, she didn't answer him, she just knitted her fingers tightly together as if she didn't quite know what to do with her hands.

"Kate could probably use your support. She is a little overwhelmed by all this."

She blinked at him and he thought he saw disappointment there.

"Oh. Of course. Kate."

He reached for one of those hands, untangling it from the other so he could squeeze her fingers. "And I want you there, Taylor. I want to share this joy with you just like I want to share every other joy in my life with you."

"What—?"

"I love you, Taylor. I've been trying to tell you that for a while now but I can never seem to find the right words."

Her gaze flew to his and he had to admit, relief coursed through him when he saw the emotions that chased across her features—shock and wariness and then a slow, hesitant wonder.

"Those three are enough," she murmured, and stepped into his waiting arms. "More than I ever dreamed of hearing."

"I love you," he repeated. "I think I've loved you from those early days of the trial, when you stood by your brother, tall and loyal and courageous. Even though the rest of the world turned on him, you never gave up."

She framed his face with her fingers and kissed him with a sweet tenderness that sent every other thought in his head scattering.

Several moments later, when his head stopped spinning, he gave her one more swift, fierce kiss, then stepped away. "When I arrived here last night and thought you were lying somewhere bleeding and hurt up on that mountain, I think I stopped breathing. Everything inside me seemed to seize up. When I think about what could have happened to you up there, I'm sick."

"I could only think of two things when I thought Martin was going to kill me—that no one would ever know Hunter was innocent, and that I'd never have the chance to be in your arms again, to tell you how much I love you."

He groaned and pulled her to him. He wasn't sure if his poor heart could contain any more joy—first finding Charlotte after all these years and then finding this woman. His brave, beautiful, incredible Taylor.

"Will you come with me to Liberty, Taylor?"

She smiled that soft smile he loved so much and he decided his heart could always find room for more.

"Of course," she said. "And anywhere else you want to take me."

Epilogue

"Stop fidgeting with that tablecloth, Taylor. I promise, everything looks great."

"Great isn't enough," she told Wyatt, one eye on him snatching olives out of a bowl and one on the table bulging with food. "It has to be perfect."

He laughed and gave her a quick kiss on the forehead. "The man has been incarcerated for thirty months, two weeks and three days. I don't think he's going to mind if the folds of the tablecloth aren't just so."

She pressed a hand to her fluttery stomach. "I'm nervous. Why am I so nervous?"

"Because he's your brother. Because you love him. Because you want to make everything he's been through disappear with a snap of your fingers and one fancy dinner. You can't, though, Taylor. You know you can't. His prison time will always be part of who he is, just like everything you've been through helps make up the incredible woman I'm crazy about."

She sighed and slipped into his arms. "You're not supposed to be so smart," she murmured against his mouth.

"I know. It's a curse." He grinned, then kissed her.

It had taken longer than she'd hoped to free Hunter. A week had passed since the night Martin tried to kill her. In that time, Nick Sinclair had been working feverishly behind the scenes to have Hunter's conviction voided and to see him walk free.

Today was the day. Though Taylor had wanted to be standing outside the prison doors with banners, noisemakers and a big brass band, that wasn't what Hunter wanted. He had asked her to stay here at their family cabin in the canyon.

He wanted no celebration at the prison, he said. He just wanted to walk out those doors quietly, unnoticed, and slip into the car Sinclair had arranged for him. He wanted to drive himself here for their reunion and a small dinner with the few friends who had stuck by him.

As hard as it was waiting for him, she knew she had to respect his decision. For two and a half years Hunter had had little control over his world. She wouldn't take this small victory away from him.

"Is he here yet?" Kate asked from the doorway, and Taylor tugged her mouth away from Wyatt's.

"Not yet," Wyatt answered, smiling at his sister, though he kept Taylor in his arms.

"Nick called and said Hunter left the Point of the Mountain about twenty minutes ago. He should be showing up any time now."

Kate sighed and wandered to the window. Wyatt followed her progress, as he always did. Whenever they were together,

Wyatt couldn't stop looking at her, as if he still didn't believe she could really be there. Gage was the same way.

Taylor didn't mind—she found it terribly sweet that these two macho men could turn so gooey over the little sister who had been returned to them. She knew Kate wouldn't mind it either eventually, but for now, her friend was struggling to deal with all that had happened, to build a tentative relationship with the family that had been stolen from her.

Kate was undoubtedly Charlotte McKinnon. Follow-up DNA tests had proved it without a doubt. And while Kate accepted the physical proof, Taylor knew her friend was having a difficult time coming to terms emotionally with the sudden shift her life's journey had taken.

It was hard for her, Taylor was sure. Though Wyatt and Gage and their parents had kept their love for little Charlotte alive in their hearts, they were strangers to Kate, people she hadn't known existed until a week ago. She couldn't be expected to fit right in to their family overnight as if those twenty-three years apart had never been.

It would come, Taylor knew. Once Kate had time to adjust, she would grow to love them.

"I hate this sweater," Kate said after thirty seconds of staring out the window with the restlessness that had been a part of her for the past week. "I think I'll go change."

"Again?" Taylor asked with baffled laughter in her voice. Kate usually didn't pay any attention to her clothes but she had already changed sweaters twice.

"You know, I'm sorry for what Hunter has been through," Wyatt said after Kate left the room. "But if Dru and Mickie had never been murdered, Hunter wouldn't have gone to prison and I would never have met you. If I hadn't met you, we would never have found Kate."

Ripples and waves, she thought. One event touches off a chain reaction that changes lives forever.

She hated what Hunter had endured but she couldn't bear the thought of never having Wyatt in her life, or the hole that would never have been filled if the McKinnons hadn't found Kate.

She wondered if Hunter would find comfort that at least some good had come from his ordeal.

"I love you," she murmured, savoring the heat and tenderness her words sparked in Wyatt's eyes. His return kiss held love and joy and promise.

A moment later, they heard the sound of a car pulling up outside, then the slam of a door. Her stomach tied itself in knots again.

"There's your brother," Wyatt said. "What do you say we go welcome him back to the world."

It was the perfect thing to say, she thought as those knots untangled again. Taylor smiled at this man she loved so much, then grabbed his hand and walked out into the sunshine.

* * * * *

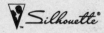

Silhouette Desire

Coming in November 2004 from

Silhouette Desire

Author Peggy Moreland presents

Sins of a Tanner

Melissa Jacobs dreaded asking her ex-lover Whit Tanner
for help, but when the smashingly sexy rancher came
to her aid, hours spent at her home turned into
hours of intimacy. Yet Melissa was hiding a sinful
secret that could either tear them apart,
or bring them together forever.

The TANNERS of TEXAS

**Born to a legacy of scandal—
destined for love as deep as their Texas roots!**

Available at your favorite retail outlet.

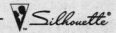

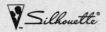

COMING NEXT MONTH

#1327 ALONE IN THE DARK—Marie Ferrarella
Cavanaugh Justice
Patience Cavanaugh felt relieved when detective Brady Coltrane agreed
to find the man stalking her. But there was just one problem. Brady
was irresistibly sexy—and he wanted more than a working relationship.
Even though she'd vowed never to date cops, he was the type of man to
make her break her own rules....

#1328 EVERYBODY'S HERO—Karen Templeton
The Men of Mayes County
It was an all-out war between the sexes—and Joe Salazar was losing
the battle. Taylor McIntyre tempted him to yearn for things he'd
given up long ago. Would their need to be together withstand the
secret he carried?

#1329 IN DESTINY'S SHADOW—Ingrid Weaver
Family Secrets: The Next Generation
Reporter Melina Becker was 100 percent sure Anthony Benedict was too
potent and secretive for his own good. His psychic ability had
saved her from a criminal who was determined to see her—and her
story—dead. They were hunting for that same criminal, but Melina knew
that Anthony had his own risky agenda. And she *had* to
uncover his secrets—before danger caught up to them!

#1330 UNDER THE GUN—Lyn Stone
Special Ops
He could see things before they happened...but that hadn't saved
soldier Will Griffin from the bullet that had killed his brother. Now
he and fellow operative Holly Amberson were under the gun. With
his life—and hers—on the line, Will would risk everything to stop a
terrorist attack and protect the woman he was falling in love with....

#1331 NOT A MOMENT TOO SOON—Linda O. Johnston
Shauna O'Leary's ability to write stories that somehow became reality
had driven a wedge into her relationship with private investigator
Hunter Strahm. But after a madman kidnapped his daughter, he could
no longer deny Shauna's ability could save his child. Yet how could
he expect her to trust and love him again when he was putting her
in jeopardy for the sake of his child?

#1332 VIRGIN IN DISGUISE—Rosemary Heim
Bounty hunter Angel Donovan was a driven woman—driven to
distraction by her latest quarry. Personal involvement was not an
option in her life—until she captured Frank Cabrini, and suddenly
the tables were turned. The closer she came to understanding her
sexy captive, the less certain she was of who had captured whom...
and whether the real culprit was within her grasp.

SIMCNM1004